The Final Voyage of Avery Mothmere

The Final Voyage of Avery Mothmere

Helen Whistberry

Other Books by the Author

To LA and Ian for their encouragement
and to my sister who set my feet upon the path

Contents

The Doomed Ship

Far below the ocean's surface, a horned beast waits and watches. It grinds its teeth and snorts sparks of lava-fueled fire into the chilly waters. Listens to a sailor's shanty warbled above the waves. A catchy tune. It taps one clawed foot to keep time and makes plans to join that unfortunate crew.
—excerpt from A Naturalist's Observations of an Oft-Neglected World

THE WOOD BENEATH MY feet creaked and moaned like a dying animal. I had lost my last pair of shoes overboard in the tumult of the latest cyclone we'd endured and must suffer the cold, splintered decking with no protection but the thin black stockings that were currently more holes than whole. I did not complain. With most of the crew dead or dying and I capable of but little assistance, the best I could do was make myself even smaller and quieter than was my want and keep out of the way.

"A voyage of the damned," the Captain had muttered only this morning over our hasty breakfast of smoked cod and stale, saltwater-soaked biscuits. He was bitter and worn thin from misfortune followed by calamity on top of disaster. Many were the hard glances sent my way. A modern-day Jonah, he was thinking perhaps, though he did not dare speak it aloud, for such words invite their own bad luck.

I would be hard-pressed to argue the point, for by the crew's own accounts, *The Serendipity* had encountered calm seas and felicitous winds before my companion and I came aboard at its last port of call. Poor Mitra. She was terrified of sailing, having dreamt many times of her bones clapping and knocking about together on the lonely ocean floor like rolling dice. Had she the Sight after all, as she so often claimed? For such was indeed her fate.

When I closed my eyes, I saw her still. The almost comically surprised expression on her face as the wrathful wave caught her about the waist and dragged her through the cruel railings, splitting them both in twain. Her top half went one way, the bottom another. I tried not to picture their slow descent, the churning water pulling at her skirt of plain stuff and ripping the pins from her dark curls. The obscenity of her innermost secret parts sprawled open, convenient for sharp-toothed marine creatures to begin their relentless feast.

How long does one's mind continue to conjure sensible thought in such a predicament? Not long, I hoped. The only thing worse than witnessing the breaking of her body would be to think she was aware of what was happening and counting out her losses as she drowned. My scientific mind told me that the shock of her injuries would have shut down any sensations of pain or despair in an instant, but my imagination couldn't help but run wild, fancying her reaching out one hand to catch at a passing foot so they might not be parted in death.

My father always rebuked me for my morbid fancies, so I learned early not to speak of them. But one soon discovers that to constantly guard one's tongue is a tiresome affair. Far easier not to speak, though I would be hard-pressed to decide if the world was more suspicious of one who talks too much of what is deemed nonsense or one who talks far too little. You might almost think conserving one's words was itself a crime. I had hoped to escape such societal expectations when I traveled, but it turned out even the roughest and most graceless of sailors demanded the social niceties from one of my station.

As I huddled close in a small alcove that I'd discovered behind the water barrels lashed to the deck, I heard the Captain shouting orders barely audible above the indescribable commotion of the oncoming storm. I must admit a part of me found the experience restful. At that moment, I required nothing of anyone, and no one required anything of me. To cling, to survive, to speculate how long the ship could withstand yet another tempest with its greatly reduced crew and damaged hull—that was all. To find my life and its striving reduced down to this simple calculus was a relief. For once, I felt my over-busy brain settle and focus.

A dozen men lay below in their hammocks, too ill of the fever to assist or care whether we survived our current trial. Some might even welcome the ship foundering, dragging them down with it and putting them out of their endless misery since they were bound to succumb to their symptoms as had so many others. Another five sailors had been washed overboard as dear Mitra was. That left a scant rollcall of hands aboveboard.

The cook had been installed before the wheel, being the only one remaining who was big and strong enough to fight the inexorable pull of the waves. He looked frightened to death, poor man, and I couldn't help but think he was steering the ship more or less at random. He lacked the talent of seamanship and would have been far more comfortable stirring a pot on the woodstove in the galley below. The Captain should by rights have been navigating, but he was distracted helping the skeleton crew bring in the sails before they were ripped to pieces and the masts shattered.

I was soaked through and as chilled as I'd ever been in my life. My teeth chattered out an eccentric rhythm that vibrated through my skull, giving me the headache. I became aware of a warm spot at my back. It was Soot, the ship's cat, a brave golden-eyed mouser with long black fur, four white paws, and a charming little silver moustache. I turned and curled round him, sheltering him from the driving rain. I couldn't say which of us was shivering more, but what comfort it was to know even one living creature was near to me and faithful enough to share in my fate.

Never before in my travels had I experienced seasickness, but the wildly gyrating ship, the sudden ups and downs as we dropped from highest wave to deepest trough, were challenging even my iron stomach. Any thought of heaving over the side was out of the question, so I concentrated on calming my breath and conjuring pleasanter thoughts in my mind.

The Royal Gardens of Lilliash, lush green lawns punctuated by blooms rioting in every color imaginable. The orchards, tree branches weighed down with a bountiful crop. Mitra's perfect white teeth biting into a purple plum as the juice ran down her chin. Me, laughingly tucking a twig of white apple blossom behind her ear. The guard who half-heartedly chased us off with a grin and a rude observation, indulgent to our spring fancies and petty thefts.

No, it was too painful to think on Mitra. Better to recall a time from before our first meeting. The summers I spent on Grandfather's estate, wandering the forbidden wilds and helping bring the herds down from the high places where they fled to escape the spring floods in the meadows. The little wounded owl I nursed back to health and released to the sanctuary of the deep forest with the truest regret. I could feel the grip of its tiny claws round my rough forefinger still. Treasured its hard-won trust.

I'd always had a way with creatures of every kind. Maybe that was why Soot had sought me out. We'd had many a lively conversation below deck in happier times, and he rejoiced in showing off his latest kills to me before devouring them.

"Fret not, small friend," I whispered in one soft ear. "It's only another storm and we have weathered many a one these past weeks. All will be well."

Alas that I've never learned not to tempt fate with foolish predictions!

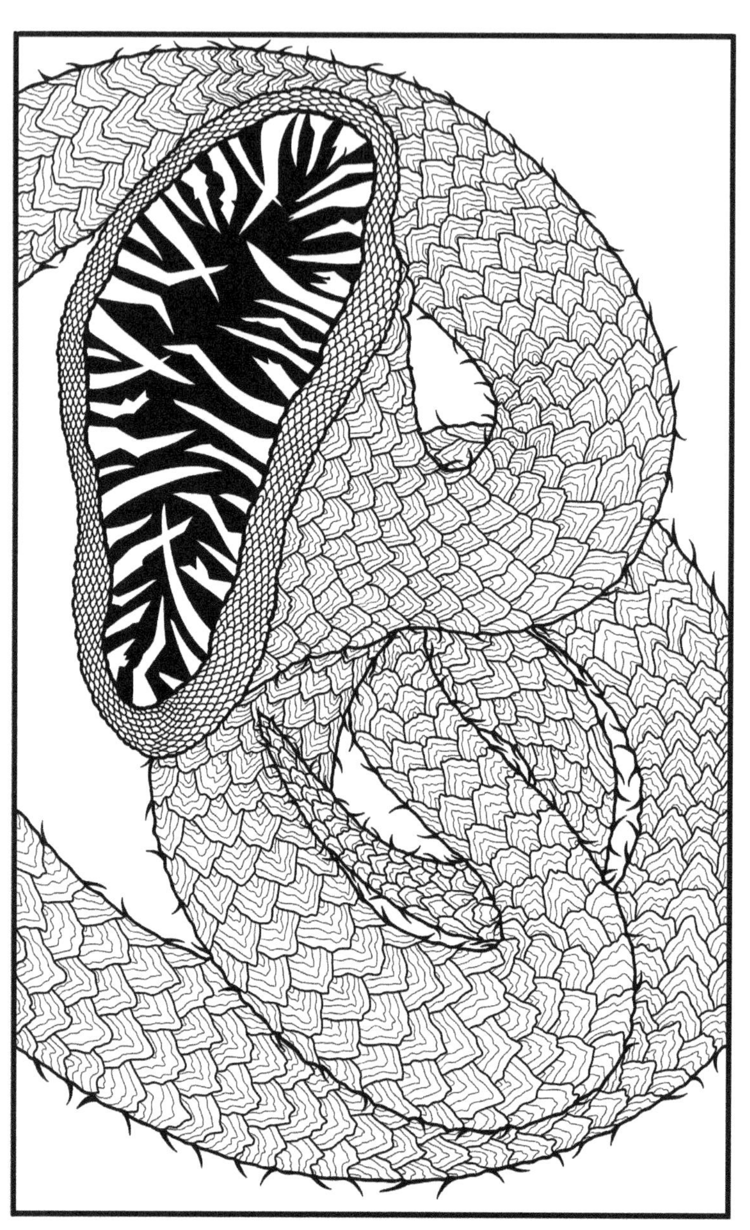

The Squirming Terror

I raced onward like a demon chasing the last sinner through the bowels of Hell, never pausing to assess the cost of my headlong plunge. Understanding only that to halt, to turn, to face the thing following me would complete my descent into grief and madness.

*   –excerpt from Memoirs of a Disgraced Magician*

I WAS EXAMINING SOOT'S face, admiring the small moustache which gave him an air of being constantly amused, when his eyes grew very big and wide and black. His size doubled in an instant as the hair on his trembling body stood on end. A screeching yowl that passed through every musical scale imaginable and seemed to have no end flew from his lungs. I turned my head to follow his gaze.

At first, I thought it must be the limb of some tentacled creature reaching up and around the ship from the depths, but then I realized it was unencumbered by any unseen body and was complete unto itself. How to describe it? Snake-like, eel-like? Neither seem sufficient comparisons for the winding, sinister thing that stretched and spiraled its way across the deck toward us.

Subtle bilious green and mustard yellow stripes ran diagonally down its form, which was twice as long as my height and as big around as my thigh. It quivered and twisted back and forth upon itself like an earthworm stranded on a stone walkway after a heavy downpour, and its jaws worked ceaselessly, showing off concentric circles of needle-thin teeth.

A tongue as long again as the creature but thin as a length of fine worsted reached out and encircled one of my ankles. Fierce pain made me cry out involuntarily, for it was much against my nature to call attention to myself even under such duress. The tongue felt rougher than the bristles of a wild pig and small pinpricks of blood appeared through the tears in my stocking. I looked about me for something that could be used as a weapon, but the restless waves had wiped the deck clean of anything not tied down.

Brave Soot advanced, clawing at the thin tongue with a ferocious swipe of one white-booted paw that severed it, leaving only remnants clinging to me. I made haste to rid myself of the awful bond, tearing my fingers nearly to pieces against the jagged tissue.

The monster—for such it seemed, no mere sea animal or fish—reared up in a fury at this outrage and would have surely struck and killed the cat if not for the Captain bursting upon the scene suddenly, massive ax in hand. He chopped the thing in two to the immense relief of the three of us there in that gruesome tableau, but our reprieve was short-lived.

Before our astonished eyes, the two pieces each doubled in size. Where once there was a single monstrous foe, now there were two.

"Catch!" the Captain cried, tossing a wooden-handled clasp knife in my direction.

Being both frightened out of my wits and naturally clumsy, I fumbled for it too late. It slid past me, and I wasted precious moments fishing about behind the water barrels retrieving it. Soot shot up to my shoulders with a screech, digging his claws into my woolen coat, which was thankfully thick enough to shield my back from injury. My hands at last found the knife and whipped it out, unfolding it as quickly as possible.

Even so, I was barely in time to sink it into the head of the creature reaching for me with its horrid mouth. Such was the force of my blow through its brain, I succeeded in pinning the monster to the deck itself. I shall never forget the awful writhing of the thing in its death throes—the slimy tail that whipped across my cheek, leaving a slick, rotten ooze that stank so, it made my eyes water.

"Pierce the head," I called out. "Don't separate it into pieces!"

But my low voice was lost to the chaos all around. I watched in despair as the Captain and two other sailors who had rushed over to help chopped at the creatures, creating more and more of them. I could not blame them. We were worn and hungry and tired almost beyond rational thought. They acted instinctively and did not notice until too late that they were making our plight infinitely worse instead of better.

We were soon surrounded by a thrashing mass of terror. Even the cook abandoned his post at the wheel to confront the emergency, making some inroads into the invasion by sweeping as many of the creatures as he could overboard with a stout, twiggy broom. Alas, the waves were intent upon undoing his efforts by throwing the worms back upon the deck faster than he could remove them.

I was not idle. Retrieving the knife, I stabbed here and there attempting to kill as many as I could, but it seemed a hopeless endeavor. The creatures chased the remaining crew around the deck. Some men jumped overboard in their panic while others disappeared under a squirming pile of monsters and blood and were not seen again.

Emerging from my previously safe haven, I was backed slowly by the relentless assault toward the bow of the ship, which was bucking and twirling in the angry whirlpools spun off by the storm. Of the rest of the ship's complement, including the Captain, I could see no sign. I was alone except for my stalwart companion, who clung to my shoulders throughout the battle with feline grace and tenacity.

Glad of the ease of movement afforded me by my borrowed, loose-fitting sailor's trousers, I resorted to climbing up the railing and backing out upon the bowsprit so I could keep an eye on my pursuers, while hoping the narrower access to my person might be to my advantage. What an extremity of emotions I endured as I clung there, lashed and nearly blinded by rain and wind, confronting an army of such horrors that I'd never dreamed of in even my worst nightmares.

My thighs ached from the effort of staying upright upon the wooden spar beneath me while keeping my hands free for defense. The creaking and groaning of *The Serendipity* was now louder even than the storm. Gaps opened in the planks of the ship—it was being torn apart. Large swathes of the worms fell below deck as cracks appeared. I could only imagine the shock and dread of those sick men below as such hellish creatures rained down upon their heads. I prayed their ends were as swift and painless as possible.

As for myself and Soot, our choices were reduced to being eaten alive by the worms or diving into the deep, where drowning would soon follow. Such was my empathy for all creatures, I felt infinitely worse thinking of the poor cat's confusion and fear than my own. I would gladly have sacrificed my life at that moment if it could have saved my companion.

My indecision might have kept me paralyzed indefinitely if the sea had not decided the matter by swamping us with one final wave of irresistible power. Huge chunks of the ship broke off and floated away or were dragged under as I clung to what remained of the bow. Trying to accept that this was the way my benighted life would end, I barely noticed at first the tugging at my ankle, but just as the bow began to sink, I was dragged down and enfolded in a pair of arms as strong as the muddy embrace of the grave.

THE SINGING BEACH

They trailed fingers through the white sand. Studied the shifting grains as it sworled and twirled. Watched the patterns change and speak until their eyes grew sore, then closed their lids and lay back in the burning cradle, sighing as the winds buried them, erasing their existence from living memory.
–excerpt from The Chronicles of Disintegration

I WONDERED AS I was pulled under the waves—*who is this and what is this final embrace?*

Mitra's face rose before me. She had always been jealous company. Had she risen up from the ocean depths to drag me down to join her? Did her spirit resent the notion I might escape her in my last moments? A fanciful idea, but then as I've said, I have always possessed a morbid and sinister view of the world and its many risks and disappointments.

All I knew for certain was that the arms holding me were hard as stone and impossible to resist. In truth, I was so exhausted and worn from grief and loss and the seemingly endless struggle for existence that I was pleased to have choice wrested from me. There is a kind of peace that comes with being stripped of options. When there is only one way left open to you, how easy it is to follow that path without the burden of questioning, always questioning whether you are doing the right thing or not.

I did spare one moment to lament Soot's fate, but then cats famously have nine lives, so I hoped he might be reincarnated into some safer existence. A place on a hearth near the comfort of a smoldering fire. The joyous laughter of children, young still but old enough to know how to be gentle and kind to the family pet. Plentiful meals of filling meats, interspersed with sweet tidbits as a treat. Soft laps for kneading and absorbing the lovely thrum of contented purrs. Such a paradise I imagined for my friend as consciousness faded.

As final thoughts go, these weren't bad ones, but—as so often in my life—I was to find I was mistaken in my presumption. These were not to be my final thoughts after all.

Coming to quite suddenly, I felt a soothing breeze caress my still slime-streaked cheek. I opened my eyes to a cloudless sky so brilliantly blue and bright, I was blinded and had to shut my lids again in pain. The ceaseless and familiar roar of the ocean was near to me, but quieter now and more regular than when we were at sea. It sounded like the steady march of waves upon a beach.

Feeling the gritty warmth of sand beneath one hand, I curled my fingers restlessly around it as the grains escaped between my fingers. Then I heard the unmistakable high clear screech of a gull. Could this be? Had we been nearer shore than any of us thought? Close enough to be washed to safety as the ship broke apart? If so, it was a miracle and one worth exploring.

I tried to sit up, only to realize I was still enfolded in a pair of unyielding arms. I struggled, looking down in confusion at my situation. The arms appeared wooden, soaked through and cracked in places. They reminded me of nothing so much as the figurehead mounted upon the bow of *The Serendipity*—a well-endowed mermaid that the sailors used to lean over and give a feel for luck. I'd always thought it a disturbing and disrespectful gesture as the poor maiden had no choice in the matter (though I, of course, kept this admonishment to myself, not being possessed of the bold and confrontational constitution I so admired in others.)

Such scruples, of course, were neither here nor there in my current situation. Though I strained as hard as I could, the arms would not budge. I looked around more widely and noted that I was indeed on a beach of some sort. Black sand, finer and softer than any I'd ever known before, spread away in both directions

I could see. My feet appeared to be pointed toward the ocean, but I could view little in that direction nor anything of what was behind me.

Unfortunately, I was able to see quite far to either side, and what I observed was not comforting. A red line was advancing upon my position from both directions. I couldn't make it out exactly, but it looked sinister. Having grown more used to trouble than I would like and having no other choice, I waited as patiently as I could, straining to decipher what could be creating such an eerie effect. Sooner than I might wish, I found out.

Crabs, hundreds of them, thousands, as deep a red as overripe strawberries and as large as my head, clacking their front pincers in an oddly soothing percussive rhythm. Their bodies bumped and snapped, one hard shell against another, adding to the cacophony of clicking. I turned my head frantically from side to side, fervently hoping these armies were intent upon each other and would some-how ignore me. Optimistic but foolish thinking, for it soon became apparent it was myself that drew them along the beach. Some uncanny sense that new prey had washed ashore within their hunting grounds.

One crab ran out before the rest, nipping a tiny chunk from my right hand and snacking on the meat delicately with its multi-part mouth. Seeing this and apprehending that the rest of me was soon to be devoured, bit by bit by bit... well, I hope you never experience such utter, hopeless horror. The sensation of what remained of my clothing being pinched and pulled, the crawling legs burrowing under my trousers and woolen coat, the small rips through my skin, the sound of snacking. I had never before screamed in my entire life—did not know I was even capable of it—but at that moment, it was the only action, the only defense I could mount.

The crabs were startled for mere seconds by the sound but too soon returned to their buffet. I tried to shut my mind down, escape to a better place in my thoughts, but the agony was impossible to ignore. Just when I thought I must go mad, a song arose from behind me. (I thought I had gone mad when I first heard it.) A high, keening sound, but with low notes that rode beneath and repeated much like the shanties the sailors were wont to sing as they went about their duties.

From the very first note, the crabs halted their fiendish attack and began to sway back and forth in time to the melody. As the tune continued, its tempo increased and the crabs followed along, undulating in their red lines as far as I could see in either direction. The vibrations their shells created filled the air with shimmer and heat. As the song reached a crescendo, I watched in disbelief as sparks flew away into the air. Ash and smoke, and everywhere these small fires, drifting up and up.

It was the crabs themselves! Some effect of the song upon them was causing them to ignite and waft away in ashy pieces to the heavens. I assumed I was delirious and hallucinating (and who could blame me after such an ordeal?) But gradually, oh, so gradually, the crab platoons disintegrated, leaving the black sands clear of my enemies. Sparks still flew about, and I watched as one landed upon the wood imprisoning me. Wet though it was, it caught at once. The spark was joined by many another as smoke thickened around me.

So, I was to end not in the depths of the ocean nor in the stomachs of a thousand greedy mouths, but in fire and flame.

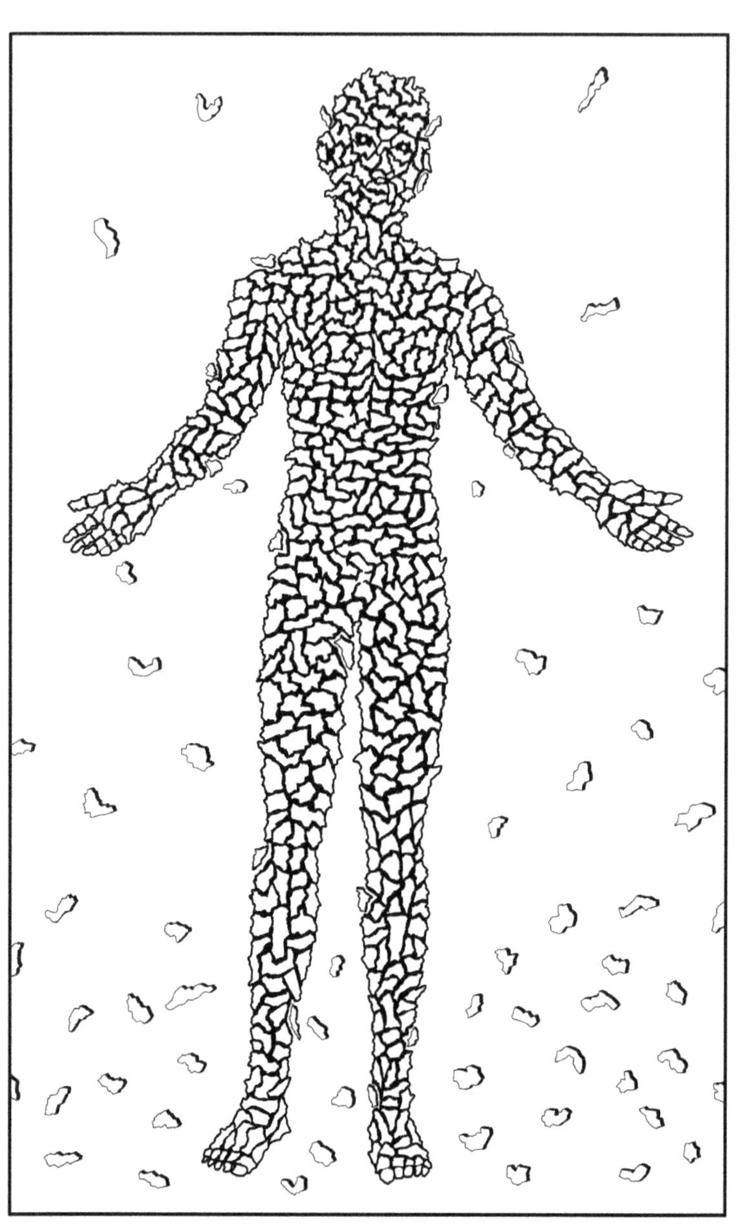

THE GILDED CHILD

I met a man in the forest who told me something of his history. Uprooted from reality, his mind had wandered a desolate landscape filled with fear, lies, and savage illusion until he heard a gentle voice call his name and followed it to a soft-flowing stream. Listening to the melody of the sparkling water, his sanity was restored.

—excerpt from A Naturalist's Observations of an Oft-Neglected World

I WAS STRANGELY CALM and numb for someone surrounded by a roaring inferno. The flames glowed with a blue light which gave the illusion of coolness, and the pressure of the arms that had trapped me gradually gave way as they burned to ash. I was able to raise myself at last from the ground and stagger to my feet, stumbling away from the fire and falling to my knees in the sand, turning so that I could confirm it was in fact the figurehead from the ship—or a faithful copy of it—burning.

The mermaid's face was turned in my direction and gave me such a smile, as though she was glad of my escape. Had she been my savior when the ship foundered? Clasped me in an embrace and floated to this shore? You may marvel that I entertained such thoughts, but I had experienced many odd occurrences in my travels. The world is full of more mysteries than most like to admit, and I'd found it to be far from the orderly, predictable, and logical place I wished it to be.

I knelt so for some time watching the mermaid until it was completely consumed. The pile of grey ash left behind blew about in the wind and mingled with the sand until it was impossible to see where one began and the other left off. The sun shone without mercy upon my bare head. On the verge of overheating, I stood and stripped my woolen coat off, finding it was the only piece of clothing that had even partially survived both the tearing claws of the crab horde and the fire.

A plaintive sound from within the thing impelled me to part the rended wool only to find a black face with silver moustache staring back at me with frightened golden eyes.

"Soot!" I cried, scooping up the damp and bewildered cat. He must have crawled within my coat on our final plunge from the ship! Miraculously, he seemed to have escaped injury. Almost unmoved by my own survival, the abrupt reappearance of one I assumed lost caused me to burst into great, gasping tears that threatened to soak the poor feline even more. He pulled away from me impatiently and bounded up the sloping beach to a field of stones beyond the sand.

I followed, astounded to find that every smooth, perfectly round stone was exactly like each of its neighbors in both size and color, a coffee-brown tone so dark as to appear almost black until lit by the sun. They were laid out in neat rows, like ranks of soldiers in formation, as far as I could see in either direction. A tall cliff face towered above us, throwing dark shadows down upon the stones closest to it. Faint echoes of the song that had driven away the crab army quivered there still, but who or what had sung it was unknown to me.

Shattered and spent, I considered turning back to recline on the softer sand, but I was now as naked as one newly born, and my fair skin was reddening quickly. As I examined my arms, I was surprised to find that, while I had many cuts and bleeding wounds from the hungry crabs as well as darkening bruising from my ordeal on the ship, I could see no evidence of any burns from the fire.

Having no wish to add to my ills by heatstroke, I reluctantly moved farther into the shade. The smooth rocks were like cobblestones beneath my unshod feet, but not unpleasant to walk upon. I approached the cliff face, examining it to see if there was any point of egress from the beach, or some sign this place was inhabited so that I might find assistance for my battered self.

The cliffs were almost as uniform as the rocks below, with smooth, black-soiled walls. Quaint white flowers grew in bunches, shooting out perpendicularly into space and drooping gracefully toward the ground. I could see no way up, but noticed Soot was stalking confidently toward an area down the way. Not wanting to lose track of my only companion, I followed.

Soot suddenly halted and looked at me expectantly, taking the opportunity to lick his paws and wipe his face (for he looked nearly as bedraggled as I must be). There, cloaked in shadow, I could just make out a stairway cut into the side of the cliff. Given the orderliness of the rest of the landscape, I was not surprised to find the steps were neatly made and all of a size—length, depth, and breadth.

I stood at the foot and tilted my head back to see how far we must climb if we were to follow this path. My heart skipped as I broke out in a shivery sweat.

There on the stairs, about halfway to the top, stood what appeared to be a child, but such a one as I could never have imagined. It held its arms open in a gesture I took to be friendly and was gilded all about with a thin, papery foil which flaked off and flew around in the wind, floating a golden mist down upon our heads. I watched as miniscule pieces caught on Soot's black fur, lending him an elegant metallic sparkle.

Raising my eyes again toward the sky, I saw that the child was now beckoning to us with one glittering hand. It turned and began to ascend the stairs, looking back often and signaling to us again and again. It obviously intended us to obey, and I, having no better plan and in desperate need of medical assistance from my many wounds and loss of blood, set my foot upon the first step.

I do not like to think back upon that journey for it felt truly endless. Soot bounded up each step easily but always turned and waited for me to make sure I was following. At first, my legs were sufficient to the task, but soon they grew so weary, I resorted to bending over and using my arms to assist. When even that became too much effort, I sat down upon a stair, slowly raising myself upon the next, while resting for longer and longer terms between each agonizing movement.

I had the uncanny feeling some beast or shadow was below us, monitoring my slow progress, though no matter how many times I paused to look down, I was unable to catch a glimpse of any such threat. I blessed many times the patience of both Soot and the gilded child, who I found always to be peering down at me encouragingly when I twisted round to look up and gauge my tortuously slow progress. At last, at last, I found myself sitting on top of the cliff face, staring around at the wide vista of the beach and sea.

From this vantage point, I could see there was wreckage from the ship strewn up and down the shore. Not only wooden planks and barrels, ropes and tangled sails, but what looked to be bodies, lying quiet, still—sprawled awkwardly upon the sand in unnatural positions.

"We should go to them," I said, entertaining the hollow fantasy that any of those motionless figures might have been as fortunate as I.

"They are gone," the child replied with such finality and assurance that I believed the pronouncement at once. Its voice was musical, thrumming with a low tone which filled me with joy. Suddenly, I knew it was the child who had sung the melody that saved me from the awful fate of being eaten alive.

"I must thank you," I began, but the child had already turned away from me and the miserable scene below and was walking rapidly away, Soot trotting at its heels.

I watched them go, eager in spirit to not be left behind, but my body had endured too much. I crawled a short distance with my last ounce of determination before giving up and lying down on my back amid the tall, cool grasses which covered this new landscape along the cliff top. Lovely wildflowers were mixed in—bright red and gold poppies, petals spread wide to catch the sun, and clusters of tiny purple blooms something like the heliotrope I knew from home.

White clouds gathered at the periphery of my vision and drifted to and fro. The shade they cast when passing between myself and the unrelenting sun was a relief to my burning skin. Now the immediate danger was past, I succumbed to my pain as a fever rose up within me, sending me shivering and sweating at the same moment. To be both hot and cold is such a peculiar, contradictory sensation. As though your body is balanced upon a knife's edge between one state of being and the next and has not yet decided which way it will fall.

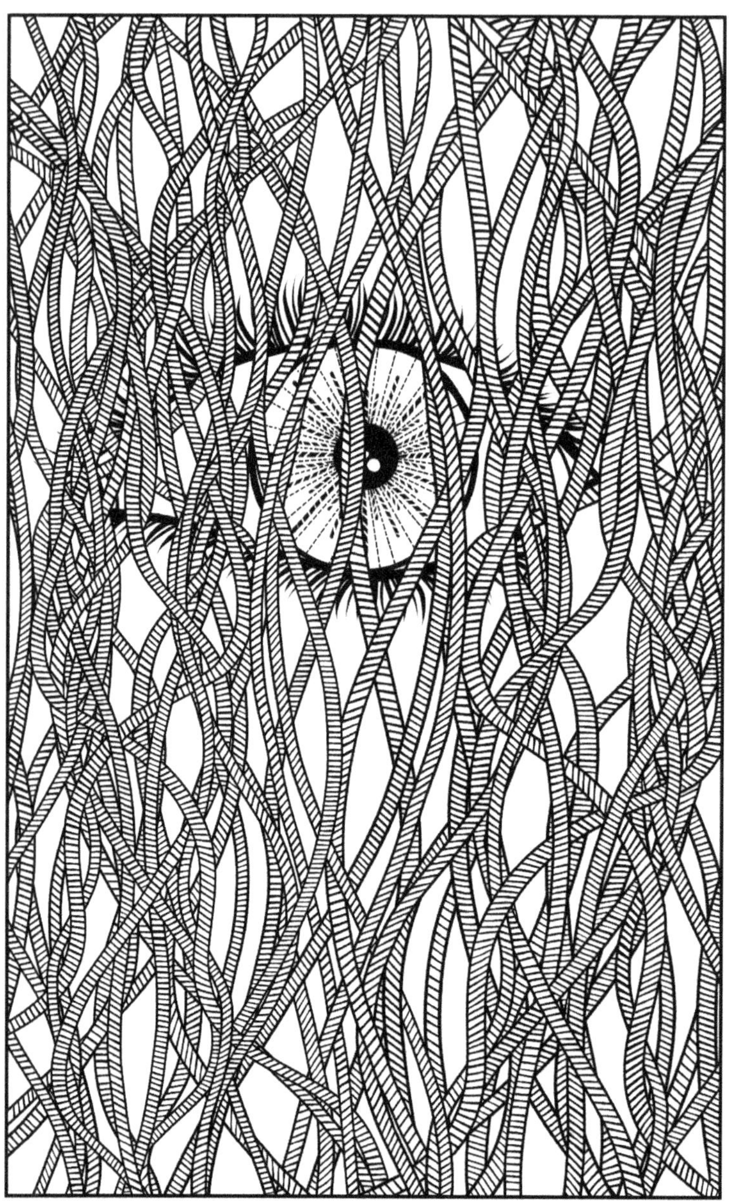

The Uncertain Countenance

To the casual observer, these beings are dull and plain, ciphers not worth the trouble of decoding and easily overlooked. Only to their most intimate acquaintances is it revealed that they are both god and goddess. Legends of arcane memory built of corrupted bone strung together with taut sinew, lost souls, and a modicum of spite.

    –excerpt from A Grimoire Malign

I WAS COMFORTABLY ENSCONCED between cool, linen bedsheets, still naked but for a multitude of bandages which hid the many outrages performed upon my person by the carnivorous crustaceans. A strong perfume suggestive of wild thyme and lemon arose as I moved my arms restlessly upon the covers, and a contraption such as I had never seen twirled round above my head, blowing a refreshing breeze upon the bed. This was most welcome, as even with the chamber's tall windows thrown wide open, the air was hot and oppressive.

The room itself was round and constructed with the same perfectly spherical rocks of the shore below the cliff. The regular and repeating arrangement of stones was soothing to the part of my intellect that was in the habit of seeking patterns in everything about me. Their dark brown surfaces gleamed as if regularly dusted and polished.

Furniture other than the bed was sparse, only a comfortable-looking armchair upholstered in buttercup yellow and a long, low wardrobe curved in such a way as to fit snugly against the curved wall. A few throw rugs in muted brown, beige, and gold tones completed the decoration. No wall hangings, paintings or even a mirror were visible, and there was no fireplace to heat the room, though if it was always so warm in these parts, none was needed.

I moved my legs restlessly with some thought of getting up and seeking out clothing from the wardrobe as I was unused to being unclothed at any time other than when in the bath. A black shape sprung up onto the bed and ran to my head, butting his own against it affectionately while purring loudly. What joy to find out Soot was still close by and that some connection remained to the shipboard life so violently wrenched from us. I reached a hand up to caress his face, wincing from the pain along my arms, only to discover that my locks had been shorn completely! My head was nearly as smooth as a billiard ball or those stones in the wall winking at me as the light shifted across their surfaces.

Finding bandages along my scalp as well, I understood it must have been deemed necessary by whoever was tending my wounds to shave my hair for better access and proper sanitation. I grieved for the dark curls which had been as black as Soot's own fur and were my one true vanity. I pondered how badly scarred my head would be and whether the hair would grow back as full and thick as before.

Scolding myself, I determined to set aside such relatively petty concerns given the catastrophes I had so unexpectedly survived. After all, though no longer strictly in fashion, there were still many wigmakers one could enlist to conceal any deficits of the follicular variety.

Soot had settled near to my right ear on one of the pillows, and the regular hum of his purrs was so soothing that I must have drifted off to sleep again. Upon my second awakening, I discovered night had fallen. The breeze from the windows was pleasantly cool without being chill. My gaze fell idly upon the large wooden door, curved like the rest of the room.

It was carved with an intricate geometric design which exerted an odd pull upon me, as though the shapes were words written in a language I had studied many years ago but could no longer quite recall. The door boasted a brass knob, patinaed green with age. I was thinking it curious that it was not kept as polished as the stones in the wall when it began to turn.

My heart raced with anticipation to meet my savior. Was it the gilded child, and would it speak more to me of who it was and in what place the remnants of *The Serendipity* had washed ashore? Or were there others here in this abode? I thought I was ready and eager for any company, but nothing could have prepared me for the sight that met my eyes.

A tall figure, stately. I got the impression it might possibly be womanly or perhaps this was simply an assumption on my part, but you will understand my confusion and uncertainty when I explain that the person was cloaked all around and from crown to foot with wavy hair of grey—not silvered but of a duskier pewter shade. The dark cloth of a gown or suit of some sort was barely visible here and there, but the surfeit of unruly tresses was truly extraordinary.

The only exposed body part was the face. Even the hands were gloved and shielded from view. And as for that face... impossible to describe. There were features there certainly, but they shifted and changed and blurred as though in constant motion or vibration. The effect was eerie beyond measure, and any excitement I had experienced at meeting my host or hostess vanished in an instant, replaced by intense alarm.

I suppose this emotion was reflected in my expression, or maybe the being was simply a Sensitive or inured to such reactions to its singular appearance, for a scratchy yet easily understood voice rang out.

"Be not afraid," it said, with the impression of a smile. "Though I am no angel, I am no devil either. You and your companion will come to no harm while you are under my protection."

It reached outside the room and pulled in a tray which must have been waiting on some table or cart beyond the door. Crossing the floor in an unnatural floating manner (exacerbated by the way the floor-length curtain of hair obscured its feet), it set the tray across my legs and gently raised my back and head, piling pillows behind so that I might sit up in comfort. Pulling off a domed cover with a flourish, the being revealed a steaming bowl of a rich-looking stew with hearty chunks of root vegetables. A thick crusty piece of bread spread thick with melting butter sat alongside.

My stomach wasted no time in reminding me it was far too empty. Regardless of any misgivings I might have, I dug in heartily as Soot tucked into a smaller dish that my host had thoughtfully provided. A glass of cool milk and a bunch of delicate pale pink grapes, each no larger than a pearl, completed the feast. We were left alone while dining, the being having glided out of the room, closing the door behind itself after revealing our meal.

Feeling much stronger after eating, I set aside the tray and pulled myself to the side of the bed. Standing tentatively, I wavered there a moment until a wave of dizziness passed. Spotting a convenient receptacle beneath the bed, I took care of the natural bodily functions before crossing to the wardrobe.

Soot padded along on his white paws at my heels like a faithful little dog, as interested in exploring as I was. The drawers were empty except for a thin robe of red silk which fit me imperfectly, its sleeves being too short and the length of the hem too long, but I was grateful for the chance to cover up my ravaged skin. It had a wide, stiff belt, embroidered in black and white silk with patterns similar to the door carvings. Although made of such light material, I found the robe was the perfect weight for the not quite chill night air and had the added benefit of not chafing and worrying against my bandages.

Unsure of what to do next, I went to one of the windows and looked out, but it was too dark a night to see any distance. Again, as it had on the stairs up the cliff, a picture arose in my mind of some dark beast following me, scaling the walls of this building toward the very window where I stood. I dismissed such a fancy as the leftover effect of the fever I had suffered, but it made me uneasy all the same.

Too restless, awake, and disturbed to be content to lie down again, I decided to take the bold step of leaving my room without invitation. I lay one hand upon the doorknob, surprised to find it was warmer to the touch than I would have expected, but it turned easily enough. I was not locked in as I'd half expected from having read far too many of the latest thrilling novels.

Outside was an open landing with a small wooden table and bench. Steps led downward in a spiraling, swooping staircase. None led up so I deduced I must be at the top of whatever dwelling this was. A tower perhaps? The circular shape of the room suggested such a structure. Soot and I ventured down, my robe trailing softly behind me.

Round and round we went. I soon expended whatever small reserve of energy I had recovered, but as it was less effort to continue down than attempt to reclimb the steps to my room, I gritted my teeth and carried on. The clinging skirt of my robe became more irksome and cumbersome the wearier I became. It was nearly inevitable, given my native lack of grace, that I would manage to tangle my legs up in the red silk.

I plunged headfirst into the unknown below.

The Imprecise Translation

There is a vault hidden at my core, in the deepest, most secret place of my heart. In it is a single sheet of pale blue paper, a note to myself that would solve the mystery of me. I have never read it and never will. Some things aren't meant to be known.

—excerpt from Memoirs of a Disgraced Magician

There was barely time to chide myself for my talent at misfortune before I was caught in strong arms and held to a breast rendered invisible beneath a cloak of grey. I had thought I would be disgusted to be held near to that unnatural abundance of hair, staring up into a face which refused to resolve itself into any definite features. I have never been fond of touch, whether hugs, kisses, or a hearty handshake, but the sheer relief of being saved from a devastating fall overcame my usual distaste.

I was impressed with the being's strength (for I am no lightweight). It carried me as though I was but a child. This thought reminded me of the gilded figure from the cliff, and I wondered again if they were also a resident of this house and whether I would meet them once more.

The rest of our downward progress passed uneventfully, and I was deposited with gentleness and care on a forest-green velvet sofa in yet another round room. This one was much larger than the bedchamber above and more richly furnished.

Matching green curtains framed the windows that ringed the room. A set of glass-paned doors led, I presumed, to the outside. Glowing landscapes and delicate paintings of flower arrangements and other still life subjects adorned the walls. (Portraits were notable by their absence.) Comfortable chairs and sofas abounded, and a modestly-sized circular table of dark mahogany wood with four matching chairs provided a place for meals or a game of cards. I wondered whether this extraordinary individual even indulged in such mundane pastimes.

"Thank you, again," I said, as it hovered in front of me, moving its gloved hands in a restless wringing motion that might have indicated worry or anxiety in any other being. "I'm afraid I'm nothing but trouble for you."

"You have suffered much. I am pleased to help you. We do not get many visitors here, though I am often called away on visits of my own."

As it spoke, the gilded child suddenly emerged from behind it. The being put its hands upon the child's shoulders as though laying claim to it. The child's appearance was much subdued indoors without the sunlight glinting off its golden skin, but in some ways, the effect of the papery foil covering it was even more unsettling. It reminded me of an ancient corpse I'd seen once in my travels to western lands, covered in cloth wrappings, frayed and unraveling, and I couldn't help but gawk at the weird pair in what, I'm afraid, was an unacceptably boorish way.

Hoping to cover my confusion and bad manners (and also tired of thinking of them as "the being" and "the gilded child" in my mind), I decided introductions were in order.

"I am Avery Mothmere, and this is Soot," I said, indicating my friend who had curled up into a ball on my lap and promptly gone to sleep.

"Greetings, Avery Mothmere and Soot," the being replied with a courtly bow. "My name would be impractical for you to pronounce in your language. 'Theda' would be the closest to that which those I am intimate with call me."

"I am pleased to meet you, Theda," I said. "And the child?"

"Ah, the child. They do not like to share their name, but I call them—" There followed a string of syllables of such grating, discordant sound that I shudder even now thinking of it. "In your tongue, I suppose this could be something like Anchor."

The name was rather portentous for a child covered in metal, but maybe something was lost in the translation from such an arcane language into my own more mundane one. In any case, I knew it was discourteous to not simply acknowledge their names as given. "I see. Good evening, Anchor."

The child nodded solemnly.

I had, of course, a thousand other questions in my mind—most pressingly, what were these two remarkable creatures? While humanoid in form, they did not seem entirely human, yet they were not like any monster or mythical being of which I had ever heard or read. As I've said, I was not unused to unusual experiences in my extensive journeying, but my present hosts would have been at the top of any list I made in future of bizarre sights.

"Forgive me for asking," I said, compelled by an insatiable curiosity which overwhelmed my fear of offending either of them, "but are you male or female?"

Theda cocked its head to one side very much like a canary I once kept in a silver cage. "Is it important?"

What could one say to that? I'd already crossed the bounds of propriety by being so inquisitive. "I suppose not. Please excuse me."

"It doesn't matter. We are used to the strangeness of your kind."

I longed to ask what they thought my kind was but had grown shy of inquiring further, even though Theda's rebuff of my previous question had been most gentle. I decided to continue to use "it" for Theda and "they" for Anchor, though I'd no logical rationale for these choices. But I did incline toward order and precision in speech and thought, so this decision eased my mind to some degree.

An involuntary yawn interrupted my reflections. I made haste to cover my mouth, but Theda just chortled, a low chuckling sound that made me smile.

"You are worn. Rest here. Anchor will tell you a story to pass the time."

A firm hand on my shoulder encouraged me into a more comfortable reclining position on the sofa. Soot grumbled his displeasure at having his own cozy berth so rearranged but soon settled down again atop a thin gauzy cover Theda produced from somewhere. It was as delicate as a dragonfly's wing but somehow provided just the proper protection from the night air.

Anchor stood at the foot of the sofa where I could easily watch them. Their hands were clasped in front of them, for all intents and purposes like a child giving a school recitation. I was glad of the chance to hear their voice again. It was both musical and soothing. I soon closed my eyes as I attempted to picture the images they described in my mind.

I have struggled since to recall the story—though I know it was thrilling beyond measure at the time—but I felt, even as I listened, that the details were slipping through my memory faster than I could catch and store them there.

A red-feathered raptor with ice-blue eyes. An elderly couple, foreign to me in appearance and dress, huddled together under a crude shelter in a birch wood. An impossibly large bloom which unfolded one satiny purple petal and then another, but infinitely slowly. Murderous toads that rained from pink skies, gap-mouthed, tooth-rich, and intent upon destruction.

It seems to me that the tone of the tale grew more and more dire and disturbing as it went on, and yet, contrarily, I grew ever more relaxed. Long after I fell asleep, I dreamt I heard the golden voice still, dropping eldritch words through the surface of my mind like pebbles into a pond, and the ripples they made were just as lovely.

The Welcomed Guest

Within the den, a fox—ancient by the measure of her kind—licks her wounds and counts her scars. Each one is a mark of honor, a reminder she has done what was needed to survive. This may be the last midwinter she ever sees. Light and dark are out of balance and the forest lies silent under a fresh fall of snow, but she is well-content.

—excerpt from A Naturalist's Observations of an Oft-Neglected World

MY EYES OPENED UPON a new day, if the light streaming through the windows was any indication. I pushed aside the gossamer cover and arose from the sofa, feeling rested. Pulling the silk robe back into position and tightening its belt, I was drawn to the now-open double doors which led out to a patio made of the self-same round stones as the rest of the structure. I speculated whether there was no other building material to be found in the vicinity, or if this was simply the architect's preference. There is no denying it made for a pleasing effect.

A cast-iron table of fancy scroll work displayed a bountiful feast of fruit and nuts in yellow and blue bowls, crystal cruets full of syrup and honey, and a gruel-like porridge that did not look promising, but which I was to discover was delicious. There was a single place setting and chair, which I took to mean I would be breaking my fast alone and needn't wait for other company out of politeness.

The view was charming, a vast hodge-podge of tall, colorful flowers which reminded me of the disorganized cottage gardens of home. Some of the blooms were familiar—I spied humble white daisies and purple delphinium, for instance. But there were many more unknown to me, such as a delicate spiky-petaled bloom the indefinable color of a shard of broken glass that has been washed at sea until it is tumbled smooth and glows softly blue-green.

Insects buzzed busily, as they are wont to do, and as with the flowers, some I knew and others not. A fat bee bumbled close to the table, knocking against my glass of juice before continuing on its way. What I took at first to be a damselfly lighted upon the table, but its body was too short and stout, though its wings were similar to others I'd studied.

And the birds! Too many to describe here, but I spied many sparrow and finch-like creatures, though of more colorful plumage than I was used to. A larger bird, vermilion-feathered, sported a tail twice the length of its body and sang a most melodious tune, and I thought I caught glimpses through the flowers of heavier, earth-bound birds with rounded bodies and elaborately coiffed heads. (And if I imagined I saw some darker figure there as well, the pure, clear sunlight soon chased away such shadowy fancies.)

All in all, it was a not completely foreign scene, though enough of the exotic remained to remind me I was halfway around the world from my place of birth. Even though the sun was not yet high in the sky, the day was already warm enough that I was uncomfortable, sweating slightly, which caused the silk robe to stick to my skin in an unpleasant fashion. I decided to return inside and seek out other clothing before venturing farther afield, as my current ensemble was not practical for exploring and was far from what I was used to wearing in public.

It was eerily quiet as I ascended the spiral stairs to my room. There was no sign of my hosts, but I discovered a pitcher of fresh water and matching basin along with other toiletry essentials had been laid out for me on top of the wardrobe. I was struck again by the lack of a mirror, which made some portions of my morning ablutions challenging, but I persevered the best I could. Running my hands gingerly over my scalp, however, I couldn't help but be curious as to what I looked like without hair.

Many of the bandages I could see on my body were stained, showing signs that my injuries had seeped during the night, and every wound was intolerably itchy. I was tempted to pull the bandages off but didn't see any fresh ones to replace them with. I was still debating what steps to take when Theda suddenly appeared at the door, gloved hands full of clean white bandages and a bottle of some kind of ointment. Being completely naked again, I was both taken aback and somewhat mortified, but Theda simply gestured to the bed and bade me lie down so naturally and calmly that I decided any modesty on my part was foolish.

The black-gloved hands methodically removed my bandages, taking care to soak those that were sticking with water to loosen them without causing too much pain. I averted my eyes after the first one or two, shocked at the extent of my injuries. It was hard to imagine I would not be left horribly marked from head to foot, even when they healed completely.

"Do not worry," Theda said, divining my thoughts, "this balm is powerful. A potion, so to speak, of my own design."

It rubbed the lotion gently into each wound before bandaging and again, the scent of thyme and lemon arose. Unusually, I found it pleasant instead of overpowering as I was generally averse to strong aromas.

When both my back and front side had been attended to, Theda crossed to the wardrobe and pulled what I soon discovered were a white linen sleeveless shirt and pair of wide-legged trousers from one of the drawers. The material was finely woven and whisper-soft against my outraged skin. A pair of natural-colored raffia sandals completed my look. Unconventional compared to my usual raiment, but the lightness was well-suited to the warmer climate.

How did Theda stand the heat beneath that heavy cloak of hair and whatever clothing was hidden there? As it did not seem to be exactly human, perhaps it did not experience the environment in the same way one such as myself did, or it had simply lived so long in this place that it had grown accustomed to the temperature.

"You've been so kind," I said. "I don't know how I'll be able to repay you before I depart. Everything I brought with me on the journey was lost with the ship, but I can send you money after I leave here as recompense for your trouble."

"Such need not concern us. As I have said, we rarely have the pleasure of company. It makes a most unexpected but agreeable change from my usual duties."

You may wonder, reader, why I did not immediately inquire into what duties Theda had in the normal course of events, but I will confess that I still struggled with its impossible face and the all-around extraordinary figure of the being standing before me. Was I afraid? Not exactly. I got no sense of menace or hint I was in any danger. But I was... in awe, I suppose is the best way to put it. As though I had landed on Mount Olympus among the gods and goddesses I had studied with my tutor so long ago and was somehow expected to converse with celestials like they were ordinary mortals.

And so, I did not inquire. I have often wondered if it would have made any difference if I had.

THE WIDENING RIPPLE

Wait until the lilac trees are in bloom, then ford a river that churns with hope and disappointment. Cross the burning sands of regret and climb a hill piled high with restless dreaming. Search for a sign at the crossroad of memory and desire. Choose wisely but never look back. You will find what you seek on the other side of eternity.

*   –excerpt from A Grimoire Malign*

REFRESHED FROM THEDA'S TENDER ministrations, I expressed my desire to explore the outdoors further now I was more properly attired. Theda made no comment other than to stand back and indicate the open door to my room with a graceful gesture.

The ease with which I descended the stairs reassured me that my usual strength was returning rapidly. I hoped I would soon be able to remove myself from Theda's care and the trouble such an uninvited guest must inevitably cause. Regardless of its protestations that a visitor was most welcome, I was used to paying my own way and being of as little bother as possible. I knew I wouldn't be truly comfortable until I was recovered enough to continue my travels.

There was time yet to discover what transportation options this place provided. My hope was to engage passage on another ship, but I would have to write home for more funds, which would take no little time in coming. Maybe I could find a job in a local town to earn some spending money while I waited. It was not in my nature to be idle, and even aboard *The Serendipity* I had done what I could to contribute, much to Mitra's dismay. She had certain ideas about what was proper (and to be honest, some of the sailors had shared that view, but others had welcomed an extra pair of hands, particularly after their ranks were diminished by the illness that plagued us from our last port of call).

Mention of the ship may remind you of our feline friend. I will reassure you Soot was never far from my side. He followed me silently like a dark phantom, although a most welcome companion and very unlike the imaginary shadow that tickled constantly at the back of my mind and had me looking over my shoulder more often than I would care to admit.

We walked out together into the garden and discovered a winding path which led to a circle of lawn. The tips of the mown grass were brown and dry, not surprising given the unrelenting sun, but enough of the green beneath remained visible to create a pleasing effect. I looked back upon the structure we had left, eager to see it entire now that we were far enough away to gain perspective on the building.

It was a tower, as I had surmised, but instead of being straight up and down, the walls were slanted farther out at the bottom, creating an effect not unlike that of a royal pyramid if they were curved instead of sharply angled. (In geometry, the shape would be described as a cone.) Windows circled around each floor, of which I counted thirteen.

The spiral staircase was evident in the form of a leaning column along the side of the building. It was quite a feat of engineering that the stairs inside were perfectly upright rather than inclined. I puzzled over it for a time before deciding there must be some architectural trick with which I was unfamiliar behind the effect.

My room must be at the very point of the cone, though the interior ceiling of it was flat, making me curious if there was something even higher but out of view of my room. Most dwellings do have an attic, but if so, I had seen no obvious means of access to it. I was growing insatiably curious about both the tower and my hosts, but given my reluctance to ask questions, quiet exploration seemed the best option for the time being.

The stone patio encircled the tower, then the garden round that and the wide strip of lawn surrounding all. I couldn't help but think it must look something like an archery target if one could see the property from above, with the tower itself as the bullseye.

Soot and I crossed the lawn to find a low wall made again of the same round stones as the beach. I wondered which direction I should walk to find the steps down to the shore again. The thought of the bodies we'd left lying there weighed on me. While not exactly friends, the sailors had been my companions for many long weeks, and I thought they deserved some better dignity than being left exposed to the elements and nature's scavengers.

I shivered, reminded I had barely escaped such a fate myself, and had no better defense if I were to return there alone and encounter a hungry horde again. Perhaps I would find the courage to bring the matter up with Theda or even Anchor the next time I encountered them. Being more familiar with the area, they likely knew some trick of dealing with marauding creatures other than the child's destroying song.

Deciding to put the problem aside for the moment, I examined the wall in every direction I could easily observe. There was no gate visible to me, but the wall itself was so low and narrow that I was able to easily step across it while Soot made short work of jumping. I couldn't help but question what the point was of such an easily forded obstacle and decided it was simply a decorative flourish.

Beyond the wall were what I would describe as marshlands. Soft, soggy black soil was punctuated by small ponds bursting with reedy plants and waterfowl of startling variety. Their honks and squawks were nearly deafening in places where they were thickly gathered.

I looked down at my sandaled feet in dismay, afraid I would have to turn back to avoid ruining my only pair of footwear, but Soot nosed out a system of boardwalks—rich mahogany planks laid out over deeply-seated posts. This formed an ingenious path through the wetlands, so one could traverse it without getting one's feet the slightest bit damp.

It was not only hot but humid here, and I was soon sweating mightily. I thought to give up my wanderings but was enticed by what looked to be a thick forest up ahead. As the marshlands encircled the wall and its interior circles, this forest was also planted round in a circle. I tried to imagine which had come first, the tower with the landscape planned and laid out in rings around it? Or had nature created these loops and Theda or one of its ancestors had carved out more circles within? Either way, it was absolutely unique among the many places I'd visited.

As I had expected and hoped for, it was much cooler when we reached the forest. The tree canopy blocked the merciless sun and gave instant relief to my fevered brow. I sat upon the knobby knee of a huge tree root to catch my breath. I feared I'd pushed myself too far for one who had undergone such an ordeal only a short time before, but I'd always found nature's embrace to be a most effective restorative. As I sat and contemplated, the forest nestled round me in a fond embrace, and a modicum of peace returned to my soul.

The shadows were numerous here and ever-shifting. If I was being followed by some dark thing, it would find ample nooks to hide from me. No sooner had I entertained this gloomy thought than footsteps were heard, and no ordinary ones these. The very ground trembled beneath the shock of them, and tree branches groaned as they were summarily pushed aside by unseen hands capable of super-natural strength.

Having little choice (and given my doubts about being able to outrun such a foe in my current state), I held my ground, remained seated, and prepared to face whatever new anomaly approached with as much composure as I could muster.

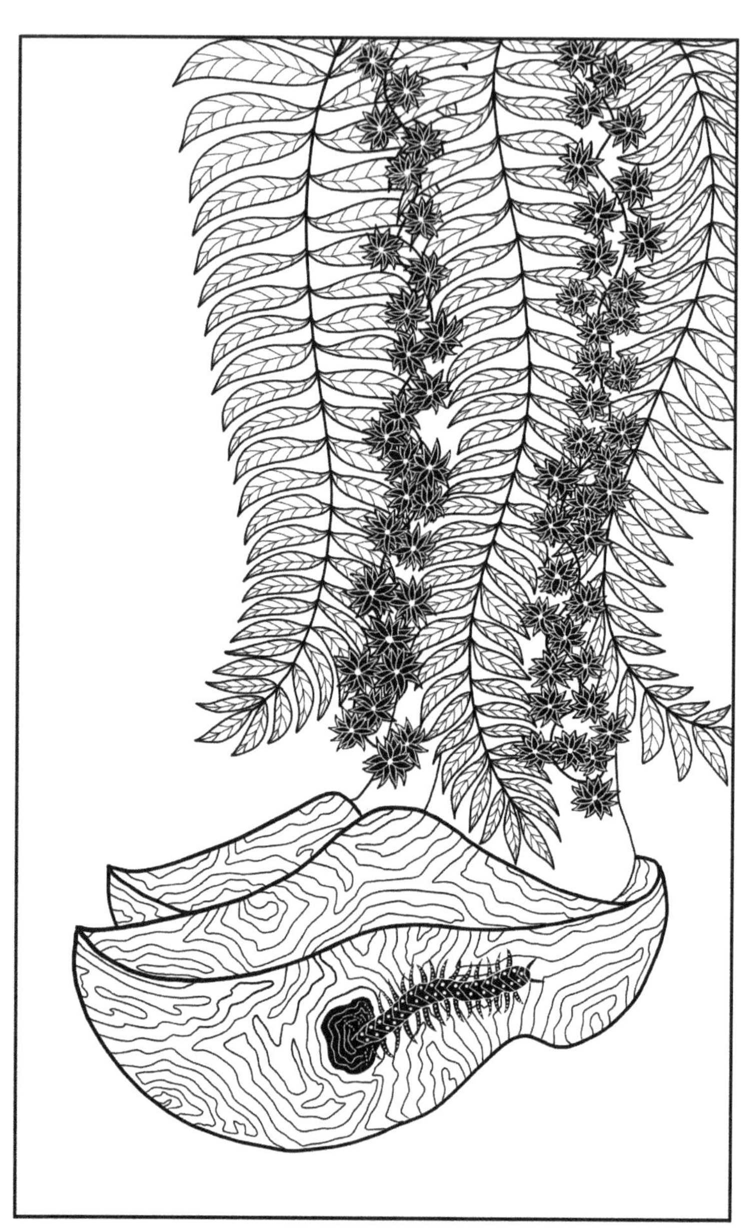

The Contemplative Giant

Shy creatures dwell in these fathomless depths, most at home in darkness. Do not approach with light or they will flee. Come at them with croaking whispers and harsh, airy kisses, unseen and barely felt. Fragile and forlorn, they will inhale this rough kindness and return it unto you a thousandfold.

—excerpt from A Naturalist's Observations of an Oft-Neglected World

"Who are you?"

It was a booming voice, accompanied by an unfortunate amount of spittle and spray which rained down upon me and Soot.

Craning my neck back, I attempted to locate the mouth so uncouth as to inflict this outrage upon us. It seemed an inordinately long way up. I had met some unusually tall individuals before during my travels, including performers who earned their bread simply by being of extraordinary height, but this one had them all bested.

I took her to be female, for she sported an ample chest and hips along with long chestnut-hued hair, generously speckled through with silver, which contrasted nicely with her dark skin and brought out the silvery-grey of her eyes. Her hair hung in unruly knots below her shoulders and served as a cozy home to a surprising number of small birds who flew in and out of nests hidden there the entire time we conversed. Her dress looked to be woven of willow or some other pliable plant, and her feet were covered by an enormous pair of wooden clogs, perhaps carved from some felled specimen of the mighty trees surrounding us.

But these interesting and unusual details paled next to her size, for she was both tall and wide, barely fitting between the forest trees, and the crown of her head was not far below the canopy above us. I was still trying to recover from this astonishing arrival, the impromptu shower, and unexpected spectacle when she spoke again.

"Terrible sorry! Been so long since I seen another soul, my manners ain't what they could be." She knelt before me and leaned over to dab at my face with an oversized green leaf. She was surprisingly tender for one so large. The leaf was both soft and more absorbent than one would expect, and she quickly wiped away the worst of her spit.

It being impossible to remain either fearful or disdainful of a gentle being willing to perform such a service, I quickly accepted her apology and introduced myself.

"I'm Avery Mothmere. My ship was wrecked upon the beach near here and I was attacked by a horde of crabs. Theda has taken me into the tower to tend to my wounds and allow me to rest and recover."

"Ah, moths be some of the most precious of children, though they do tickle if they come close. They name me Zaza, as may you. But tell me true, what be beach and ship and crab?"

Astounded one could live so near to the sea and yet know nothing of it, I did my best to explain, but Zaza looked just as perplexed as before I started.

Shaking her shoulders, neck and head, as though she was shaking off her own confusion, she said, "I never once left the forest. I'm sure there be many a thing I ain't caught sight of and don't expect I ever will, but it never yet harmed a soul to remain in ignorance of things that don't concern them. There be more than enough to study on here. No matter how many more hundreds of years I do live, I am a-doubted I could ever learn all its secrets."

"Hundreds of years?" I asked hesitantly, wondering whether the passage of time was marked differently in this country than I was used to, or if its inhabitants were just longer-lived.

"Course! I be old as the forest and the forest be old as me. We neither one can live without the other. Who would tidy the foxes' dens or teach the frogs to sing or keep watch in the small hours when a spirit be a-passing from this world to the next if it weren't for me? And who would fill my days with joy and peace and children beyond counting if not the forest? We be one and the same."

I am a most rational person and have ever sought for logical explanations for any phenomena I encountered in my explorations. Rarely had I failed to find one which satisfied my scientific nature, but this land where I had washed ashore was testing my ingenuity. Very little had made sense to me since *The Serendipity* sank—or even before, if I thought back to the endless storms we'd endured and the unknown plague. Those weird worms which had attacked us at the last. Were these nothing but some cosmic ploy to doom the ship?

And if so, for what purpose? To bring me here? I was hardly a figure of enough importance or worth for the universe to go to such lengths. Far better that Theda or whoever else was in charge here had simply issued an invitation, for I was always both too polite and too timid to turn down such offers. I had to chuckle at the absurd image of an engraved envelope and card winging its way over the waters to my berth on the ship. Given the strangeness of everything here, it would probably have been written in ink made from stardust and delivered in the beak of a phoenix all aflame.

"Do I be peculiar to you?" the giant asked, wrongly assuming I was laughing at her words.

Anxious to allay any offense, I was quick to correct the unfortunate impression I had made. "It sounds delightful—to live here always and know its ways and the creatures who dwell within. I think you are as fortunate as I am unfortunate. If I find anything amusing, it is myself. Even when surrounded by wonder, I still search for reason and the mundaneness of the explicable. I have trained in the scientific method, you see, which means I seek out what is concrete and provable by logic, formulas, testing and the like."

"What a sadness it be!"

I chuckled again. "I didn't used to think so, but recent events may make me reassess my view of the world and of myself. You are not the first to pity me.

Perhaps I seek to hold onto reality with too tight a grip. It doesn't leave room for magic and the miraculous."

"But the world be magic! And there ain't one thing we can see nor touch but be a miracle!"

"I wish I shared your vision and belief, but such has not been my experience of the world. I feel sure even this place will have some explanation. If I stay in the tower and converse with its inhabitants long enough, the questions which now harass my mind will be answered, and its secrets will be laid bare."

"Sounds foolish to my own thinking. Who'd wish to go and spoil the beauty of a mystery?" Zaza replied.

Such was the infinite sympathy and kindliness both in her expression and words that I was ashamed I had not her faith, and any counter arguments I might think to offer died unsaid upon my tongue.

The Civilized Metropolis

They carve the massive walls of sandstone with acid tears that droop and swirl, meander and hiss. What the final image will be, they cannot say. Will it speak of heartache or hope, horror or exultation? All and none. The message will be in the eye of the beholder. It is not the artist's place to tell the observer what to think or feel.

—excerpt from The Chronicles of Disintegration

"Go on to town," Zaza suggested. "You'll be finding souls like-minded to you there. Those what live in town away from natural things take a more ordinary view of the world than us as don't."

"Is there a town near?" I asked, surprised, for we seemed so far removed from any kind of civilization.

"Sure and certain. I mayn't leave the forest, but I see it from my doorstep right enough!" She laughed heartily like she had made a great joke. Not wanting to be impolite, I smiled and nodded even though I didn't understand the jest. "I'll show it you. Ain't so far as you might think."

I soon discovered she was right. Though the forest was large in circumference, it was not as deep in width as I had imagined. A very few steps for the giant, though rather more for me and Soot, brought us to the edge where a field of golden wheat lay between us and the town. Looking to right and left, I was again struck by the fact that these two further features of this unique land were also laid out to fit the circular pattern of the inner rings.

"Does the town go right around as well?" I asked.

"Circles within circles within circles," Zaza replied. "Circles within circles within circles," she repeated with a wink and a conspiratorial look as if she thought I would catch some hidden meaning in her words.

"I see," I said, loath to admit I had no inkling of what she might be insinuating.

"Hurry you both along now. This day be a-flying, and you must go and come again through all these places that be strange to you if you wish to be at tower again by fall of night. Now, if you need a morsel to eat, ask after Jack Scrabbin. I hear his'n the best pies. The birds catch at the crumbs that fall to ground and fly to tell me of it. If you be baffled and in want of help, ask for Hettie Toloch. The mice tell me she be kind-hearted. Keeps an eye out for those what lose their way."

"Thank you. I hope Soot and I will see you again on our return journey?"

"May be so, may be not so. I've my own rounds to make. Round and round and round and round." With these cryptic words and still chuckling as if she had made a witticism much to be admired, the giant strode away through the trees.

"Well! What an extraordinary encounter! What do you think, Soot? Shall we carry on or go back?"

My query was answered promptly by the sight of my feline friend slinking away into the field.

The temptation of a new environment to explore (and the chance to possibly gain some much-needed insight into this country) persuaded me to follow, wading through the waist-high wheat which brushed against my bare arms, tickling such of my skin as was unbandaged. I looked back from time to time, convinced a figure lurked, watching me from the shadows of the forest—a prickling along the back of my neck telling me it must be true while my rational mind argued the point.

Fortunately, in a very little time, we reached the edge of the town and I quickly forgot my fears, distracted by a feast for the senses. A wide cobblestone road adjoined the wheat field. Beyond, a generous sidewalk lined with rows of two-, three-, and four-story buildings crowded together with no space in between the ones I could see. I was not surprised to find that the road, the sidewalk, and the buildings were constructed from the same round stones as I'd observed on the beach and at the tower.

Their orderly shape contrasted with the sometimes higgledy-piggledy nature of the buildings themselves. Some leant forward so far, I was almost afraid to walk under them for fear they were about to topple into the street. Others leant back as though contemplating stretching out and taking a nap. The overall effect was not unpleasing. It spoke of a kind of quaintness and longevity. I could imagine all were perfectly straight and tall when built, but over time, had wearied of standing and were slowly succumbing to the pull of gravity.

Not a few carts and carriages traveled the road, the horses' hooves and metal shoes clattering with a familiar sound which made me homesick for my old haunts. The majority of people I saw were afoot, carrying baskets full of wares for sale or purchases from the lively shops which lined the way in both directions. The wholesome scent of baked goods and the heavy perfume of cut flowers battled with the grimier smells which arise in any densely populated area.

The people here looked quite normal, at least compared to the other personages I had met since washing ashore. Their skin ranged from as pale as my own to as dark as the giant's with equally as many different shades and combinations of hair and eye color. They were dressed in similar linen outfits as my own (much more informal than I was used to, but practical, I acknowledged, given the climate). Many of them, both male and female, wore their hair up and wound around their heads, I assumed for the same reason—for there is nothing more unpleasant than hair clinging to the back of your neck when you are overheated.

No one paid any special attention to me, though I was most self-conscious about not only my heavily bandaged arms but also my shorn head. A few exchanged friendly smiles and nods if we happened to make eye contact, so at least I was reassured I was not invisible.

One such was a hearty fellow with a thin brown moustache and a tray full of golden-crusted hand pies. The smell was mouth-watering, and remembering Zaza's advice, I stopped and asked if he was Jack Scrabbin.

"That's me! I see my fame proceeds me. None can match my offerings in all the town. White parsnips and purple carrots, red potatoes and orange pumpkin diced up just so and roasted with a little onion and feverfew. A few added spices of my own design wrapped up in butter pastry made with a touch of molasses. That's one of my secrets, you see. Try it next time you make pastry."

Given that I was not a talented cook, this tip was wasted on me, but I thanked him all the same.

"You must try one!" said Jack, thrusting a pie at me.

"I'd love to, but I'm afraid I've nothing to pay you with, for everything I owned was lost in a shipwreck."

"A shipwreck, you say? Sounds a thrilling tale, and I'll always accept a thrilling tale as payment, for such are rarer than coin around these parts."

And so, in between bites of what was truly the most delicious hand pie I'd ever eaten, I spelled out the recent events of my life, punctuated often by Jack's interjections.

"Worms twice your length and as thick as all that? Turrible, turrible. An army of crabs? Who'd of thunk it? The child! You've seen the child? And actually stayed at the tower? I never! Never heard tell of no one visiting the tower afore. You are a one and no mistake."

Though I don't consider myself a talented storyteller, being by habit pedantic and (I will readily admit) long-winded, Jack hung upon every word and seemed to feel entirely recompensed for his gift of pastry. He pressed me to take another "for your friend." I was alarmed at first, looking behind me nervously to see if the ever-present shadow I'd sensed had suddenly materialized at my back, but I realized the pie-maker was referring to Soot, who had been sat at my feet watching this exchange with hungry and increasingly impatient mien. I quickly broke off big chunks of pastry, passing them down to Soot, who wasted no time in scarfing them up.

Refreshed by this repast and the cheerful friendliness and generosity of the pie seller, I bade him a most sincere thanks and goodbye before wandering off to explore some little more of the town before it grew too late. I had no intention of traveling back to the tower under the cover of darkness.

For it is in darkness that shadows like best to hide.

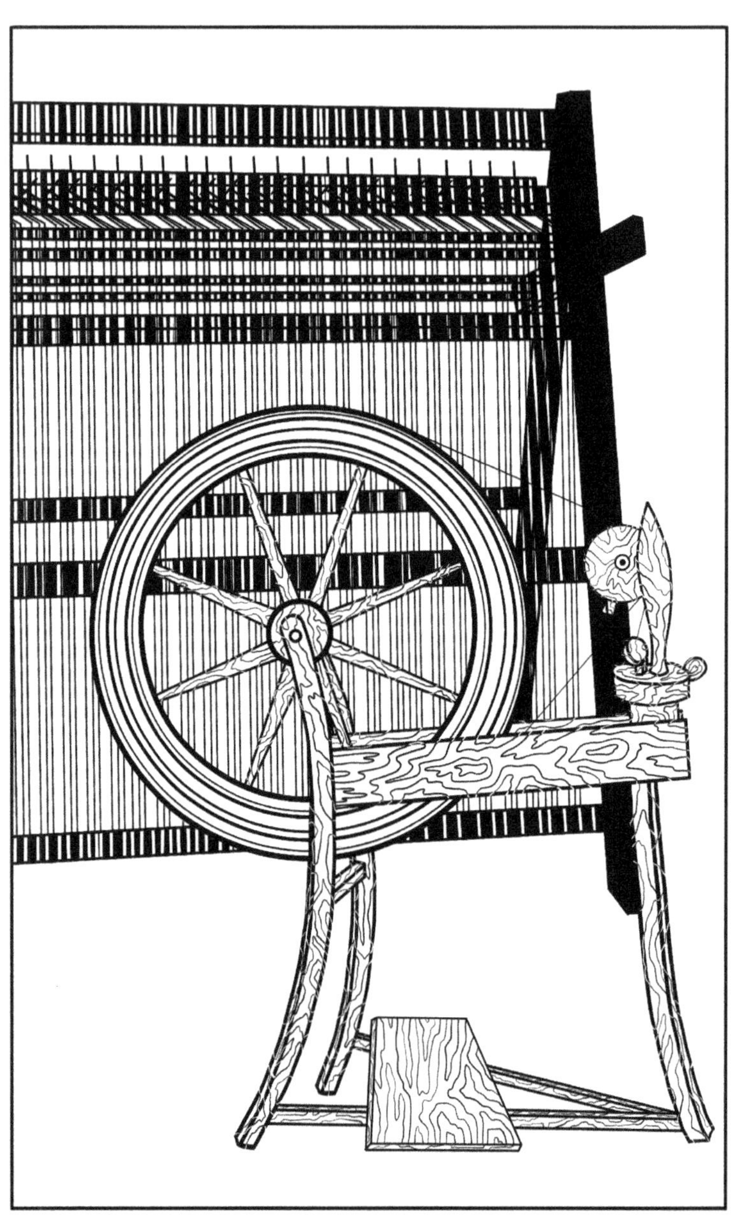

The Unexpected Question

I stitched this cloak square by square of sorrow, fear, tears, and regret. Wear it wrapped around my shoulders always. It bears them down to the earth, the impossible weight of memory. One day, I will sink below. Cover me then with this thing I have wrought so it can keep me warm among the other forgotten creatures that dwell there.

> *—excerpt from Memoirs of a Disgraced Magician*

SOOT AND I STROLLED along the single, circular street in leisurely fashion, stopping often to peer into store windows at the wares offered there. Most were as I would expect of any decently-sized town: dry goods and grocers; bookshops and furnishings; clothing stores for ready-mades and accessories, plus a surprising number of couturiers, with bolts of cloth in different colors displayed, though linen looked to be the most common. I did notice a few rich velvets mixed in at one stop and wondered if it was used for upholstery or maybe for special occasions or travel since it looked far too heavy and thick to be practical as common apparel in the local climate.

I was tempted most by the bookshops, curious to see if they carried titles from around the world or only more regional fare, and how it would compare to the literature I was used to consuming. However, possessing no purse or coin, I decided it was better not to enter—for I had never gone into such a shop in my life without emerging with arms loaded down with impulsive purchases. Besides, I wasn't sure if Soot would be welcomed and was reluctant to abandon him for even a short time in this unfamiliar place.

None of the passersby took notice of the cat though I had seen no other strays wandering the streets, nor a single person walking a dog. The sidewalks back home in a town of this size would have been full of both, so I couldn't help but wonder if such animals were foreign here, or if the idea of owning a pet was. Yet another little mystery to add to my pile.

I had taken no particular note of any landmarks as I walked. Assuming the town was another circle, it was only a matter of time before I ran into Jack Scrabbin again, or so I thought. But I was growing weary, and the sun was sinking, though I calculated I still had a few hours of daylight left. I began to regret walking so far and speculated direly on the notion which suddenly occurred to me: what if Jack had moved on with his wares before I got back? How was I to find the exact spot in the town that would lead me back to my original route?

Supposing everything was a circle within a circle, I could theoretically begin walking inward to the tower at the center from any point, but who knew if there were obstacles on other paths? I wouldn't like to find myself lost in the forest or those marshlands at night. Pondering being lost reminded me of the giant's other piece of advice, to seek out a Hettie—what was the name? It had a funny sound to it. Talon? Tilton? Tullock?

"Hello, sweetie," a kind voice interrupted my reverie. "You look like you may've gone adrift of your proper course. I am Hethian Toloch but you can call me Hettie. I'd be glad to steer you straight if I can."

Hettie Toloch—I was sure now, having heard it again, that this was the very person Zaza had recommended I seek out if I lost my way! Marveling at the coincidence, I examined the woman standing before me with avid curiosity.

She was of medium height, well below my own, and had warm coppery hair and eyes, though her hair was shot through with white strands more prevalent at the temples than elsewhere. Her figure was nicely plump, and she wore the same linen as everyone else I had seen but in a pleasant light lavender color which contrasted most attractively with her darker skin. Her hands were wrapped around the handle of a large basket that looked to contain a day's shopping.

On the verge of being thought rude for staring so long, I roused myself to action and returned her smile warmly, for there was something about her which reminded me of my own mother and her sisters, who were so much alike that they were often mistaken for triplets.

"You're correct. I'm afraid I've wandered too far. My name is Avery Mothmere and this is Soot," I added, indicating my little shadow.

"A cat! How lovely! Haven't seen one of those in ages!" she exclaimed, putting her basket down and picking up Soot. She rubbed the top of his head next to her chin and Soot's satisfied purring was audible even at distance. She somehow settled him among her purchases in the basket (though I would have sworn there was not room) and took up her burden again.

"Come along, my sweeties. I live just here," she said, leading the way to a set of stairs tucked in between two of the buildings. At the top was a door painted a brilliant cerulean blue with a knocker in the shape of a fish head with a ring through its mouth. The door was unlocked and opened easily under her hand, though it creaked mightily as she swung it in and entered.

We walked into a large open room. At the back of the space was a woodstove and kitchen nook which reminded me of the compact galley of a ship. An area that I speculated contained a bed and privy was hidden behind a cheerful flowered curtain along the left wall. The rest of the space was given over to such a jumble of things, it would take me a day or more to enumerate them all for you.

What looked to be the wheel of a bicycle (though I had seen no evidence the townspeople used such modern conveyances—I could only imagine what a bumpy ride it would be against the cobblestone street) balanced upon the statue of a small figure which reminded me of the gilded child. Vases, some of them in pieces, and an odd assortment of sticks and tree branches (to be used as firewood, perhaps?) A ship's wheel and large brass barometer hinted at a nautical inclination, while the number of books and small pamphlets would have overwhelmed even the most dedicated reader.

All of these things, as I have said, were so jumbled together that it was hard to make sense of them, but two items seemed more revered than the rest, for they stood alone and unencumbered by junk in a rare clear spot upon the floor. I recognized the first from my travels as a type of spinning-wheel. I had found this a common implement in many countries though the machines often varied in complexity and design.

This one was wooden and of the same dark mahogany which I had seen used in the boardwalk and the furniture back at the tower. It looked like it was kept lovingly polished, though it was easy to mark the places where a hand had often rested over many years. The second machine was a loom, standing empty for the moment, waiting for thread to be spun on the wheel for its next project.

"Don't mind the mess, sweetie. I'm used to it and can usually lay my hand to anything I need. Take a load off your poor feet," Hettie said, clearing the seat of a ragged wicker chair for my use. Within a short time, she had conjured up a pot of tea and a plate of cream-filled delicacies. I was glad of the refreshment after my long walk and would have shared generously with Soot, except he had curled up upon a round pillow he'd discovered among the chaos and promptly fallen asleep.

"What a lovely thing!" Hettie exclaimed, bending over to smooth the cat's fluffy tail more comfortably around him. "He looks perfectly content! And now for you, sweetie. What color would you like your shroud?"

The Golden Steed

In certain foreign parts, it is advised to lock and bar the door at sundown and remain within, for that is when the pale rider begins his rounds on his chittering stallion, eight-legged and red of eye. His faithful hound lopes beside, displaying a slathering, toothy grimace. It is said the mere sight of this fiend and his companions leaves anyone unfortunate enough to survive the encounter completely mad.

—excerpt from A Grimoire Malign

A CHILL CAME OVER me at her words. My shroud? What could she possibly mean? I must have looked aghast, for she placed one hand upon my knee, patting it reassuringly.

"Pardon me, sweetie. It may not be the custom where you're from, but here, it is our practice to weave our shrouds or have one made so we might be prepared." She busied herself in a pile of folded cloth, pulling out one after another and as rapidly discarding them, while muttering to herself. "Too dark, too light, too blue, not red enough, ah, here!"

She offered me a scrap of purple stuff, thicker than linen, finely woven and smooth to the touch. Though still shocked at the turn my visit had taken, I could not deny I was drawn to both the weave and color of the cloth. My eyes must have been deceiving me, for I thought I could glimpse silver and gold sparkles among the deep grape shade so dark as to look black unless hit by light.

"It's beautiful," I said, "but I don't understand. You mean everyone has a shroud even though they may be yet in the prime of life?"

"Of course! It wouldn't do to be caught out, would it? For things can happen sudden and then where are you—in a panic and left scrambling and working into the wee hours of the night."

"Aren't there places here which could supply you with one ready-made at need? A mortuary or other business that offers funeral services?" I stopped short, ignorant of what rites of the dead were performed in this place, for I had witnessed many and varied in my travels.

"That would never do! A ready-made shroud? The idea! We must each have one specially made, so it will fit us to perfection in every way. Stand up! Stand up!"

Too bemused by the conversation to do otherwise, I obeyed and stood still as she whipped a measuring tape from her pocket and began measuring every possible inch of me. It was mortifying to feel her hands near some of my more private places, but she obviously meant no disrespect. She earnestly jotted down numbers rapidly with a short stub of pencil on a random scrap of paper which looked to have been torn from some larger sheet.

When she was finished, she carefully wrote out my name—to check the spelling she said. "For one must understand the spelling, else all would be undone," she asserted, as though such was sufficient explanation to satisfy any questions I might have.

Still in a daze, I didn't protest as she plucked Soot from his nap and plopped him into my unresisting arms. She guided me to the door while flooding me with instructions, the two most important being to count twenty-five more houses along the circle of town in the direction we'd been traveling to find the path to the tower. The second was to return in two—"no, better make it three days, odd numbers are better"—to pick up my completed shroud.

Deciding to humor her, as she obviously meant well, I agreed and thanked her, while stuffing some of the cream delicacies into my pocket for later at her insistence. In my heart of hearts, I had already determined not to return as prescribed. Regardless of local customs, I had no wish to perceive my own shroud.

Soot was content to ride in my arms as I counted the buildings. If I was tired by our journey, I could only imagine that he, with his much smaller stature and shorter stride was even more so. He continued to look avidly around us, however, entertained by the passersby and other sights.

Nerves overcame me again as I sensed we were being followed, though as often as I looked behind, I could not mark out any one person as being a threat. Given that there was only the one sidewalk and two directions one could go—clockwise or counterclockwise—anyone behind me might quite innocently be travelling in the same direction.

"I'm being ridiculous, Soot," I whispered to my passenger. "I am tired and hurt and too hot and not thinking clearly. You must keep an eye on me so I don't behave like a fool."

Soot blinked, which I was content to take as affirmation, smiling to myself at the thought.

At the twenty-fifth building, I turned and crossed the road at a break in the traffic. The wheat stretched away in all directions, looking undamaged and un-trodden, so I was at a loss as to the exact path, but Soot jumped down and strode confidently away, quickly disappearing into the sea of gold.

Not wanting to lose him, I hastened after, catching just enough glimpses of his mostly black form to keep me guided. How welcome was the cool shade of the forest after our trek through the open fields under a still merciless (though setting) sun! To traverse the forest in a straight line toward the center was unfortunately not so simple. Again and again we were turned to this side or that by the massive trees or impenetrable underbrush.

I lost any sense of direction. For all I knew, we were traveling along the circle of forest rather than across it and might therefore wander indefinitely. It was growing dark. I felt a sense of panic at the idea of being trapped in the forest at night. At the mercy of dangers unknown, whether real or imagined, for I was ever conscious of the ghostly stalker at my back, always out of sight.

Just as I was at my wits' end, I heard a noisy bustle coming toward us from the side. I turned to face it in relief, hopeful it was the giant, who would surely be able to set us on the path once more. Imagine my astonishment to behold instead, a beast so magnificent, I could hardly believe my eyes.

It was a golden stag, towering above me, with a set of black antlers of immense height and breadth. And yet, that was not even the most extraordinary thing about the animal, for the antlers were absolutely filled with flying creatures of every variety. I tried to take inventory of them—an owl no bigger than my fist, brilliant green moths larger than my outspread hand, bats with silver fur which glittered in the light thrown off by some type of insect that glowed like tiny stars. More birds and bats of different varieties, butterflies, beetles with wings clicking and fluttering. The effect was indescribable. A constant ballet of movement and a symphony of the unique sounds each creature made.

And above them all, on the highest point of the stag's antlers, stood an iron-grey raven—a large bird and stately. It made not a sound but spread its wings wide. As if at some unheard command, the stag knelt down, unmistakably offering its broad back to me as a seat.

To say I was unnerved would be doing but little justice to my feelings. But, thinking I had few options if I wished to escape the forest and make it back to the tower before nightfall, I gathered Soot in my arms and climbed awkwardly aboard.

THE GREY RAVEN

A choir of ravens atop a gabled roof chatter. A superstitious man stops, crosses himself, thinks it an ill omen. What portents of doom are they divulging in a language too arcane for human ears? He doesn't realize they are simply discussing the weather.

*   –excerpt from A Naturalist's Observations of an Oft-Forgotten World*

THE STAG ROSE TO its full height in a graceful motion and walked equally so. I was capable enough on horseback, but this was quite a different matter, having no reins or bridle to control the beast nor saddle to cling to. I soon relaxed as the smoothness of the journey reassured me I was in no danger of falling off. The grey raven flew down to a branch of antler nearer my face and, I would very much swear (no matter how strange you think it, though no stranger than any other part of my narrative), it winked one bright blue eye at me.

Remembering the treats Hettie Toloch had pressed upon me at the last, I fished one from my pocket and crumbled it up, offering these morsels in my open hand. I was delighted to observe the bird delicately snap one up with its sharp beak as others of the flying creatures followed suit. They were all as light as could be and gentle, so rather than being frightened, I felt uniquely blessed to have experienced such trust from normally wild and wary creatures.

When the crumbs were gone, some settled back on the stag's antlers and groomed or washed themselves, while others flew off into the increasing gloom on missions of their own. Such adventures as I had undergone that day! I thought for the first time of my diary, lost at the bottom of the sea. I was in the habit of recording any unusual sights or happenings along my journey, and there had been so many in this place that I longed to make note of.

I was a competent artist and was already imagining how I might bring this stag and its rack of unusual passengers to life within the pages of a new journal, whenever I might obtain one. Perhaps I could buy one in the town, but the ugly problem of money again reared its head. I had been raised in comfortable circumstances, and my family had always provided funds for my travels, so it was a disturbing feeling to know that for the moment, at least until I could contact them, I was penniless.

This distressing reverie was broken by the welcome sight of the pointed tower, recognizable even from this distance and in the dimming light. We had reached the edge of the forest. The stag knelt again and I disembarked, sad that such a magical encounter was ending while relieved to see my destination was now so near. I was weary and aching down to my bones and had to acknowledge I'd overtaxed myself in my enthusiasm to explore this foreign land.

I turned back to speak some words of gratitude to the stag, but it was gone. All that remained was the grey raven, who hopped along at my feet, leading me to the wooden boardwalk which marked the path through the marshlands. The rest of the journey was like a dream, or a nightmare. I was so tired that I stumbled and even fell to my knees several times. With the rapid onset of darkness unrelieved by moonlight, I became even more unsure of the way and was reduced to crawling along the wooden planks for fear of plunging over the side into the water.

And ever, ever, the uncanny feeling that I was being watched by more than just my feline and corvid companions. I swore I heard the fall of footsteps at some little distance behind me, which only added to my panic and terror. What an endless time it seemed until I felt the low stone wall beneath my reaching hands. With what relief I dragged myself over and onto the wide expanse of grass.

The tower served as a beacon, as light streamed from every window. My progress was faster over the smooth lawn, and I at last reached the garden and patio which circled the base of the tower. My energy renewed to find myself so close to sanctuary, I ran to the door. It opened in a flurry, the light streaming from within blinding me for a moment.

"You have returned. You are most welcome." It was the rusty voice of Theda, cloaked as ever in its pewter-grey hair. Behind it, the gilded child nodded at me as though endorsing the sentiment. "We thought you might be lost or departed for good on the next stage of your journey."

"We did lose our way and might easily be wandering still if not for the timely intervention of some new friends. There was a kind woman in town and a beautiful stag in the forest, and this raven—" I stopped abruptly as I realized the bird was nowhere to be seen. Having escorted me safely to the tower, it had done its duty and flown back to the forest. Would I ever see it or the golden stag again? Already the memory of them was like a dream or hallucination.

Taking no apparent notice of my confusion, Theda and the child ushered myself and Soot through the tower door. Then, to my surprise but before I could protest, I was swept into Theda's arms and carried swiftly upstairs to my bedchamber, where I found an oversized porcelain bath waiting for me. Too weary to protest or pretend to modesty, I stood obediently as I was stripped of my clothes and guided into the bath.

The water was cool, slightly milky, and smelt of a dish redolent with aromatic herbs that I'd enjoyed once in a southern country. As I soaked, my many bandages loosened and floated off. Theda returned after ten minutes or so and plucked the things from the water with its gloved hands. I marveled it would risk ruining a pair of fine gloves by such treatment. Was there some reason Theda was never seen without that particular accessory?

It was all one with the weird cloak of hair and the masked face which wasn't quite a mask but was far different from any face I'd ever seen. Its features were always in motion, like the individual flittering creatures on the stag's antlers, and yet I was unable to discern any one of them, for they were vibrating too fast for the eye to follow. Was there a recognizable human mouth, nose, eyes, and cheek under this disguise? Or something so disturbing that it must be kept hidden?

I tried not to stare every time Theda came close to fetch a soiled bandage from the bathwater, but I think it could not help but be aware of my interest, a guess soon proven correct.

"You wonder about me," Theda said, a statement of fact rather than a question.

"I do apologize!" I blurted, for where I come from, to be caught staring in such an impolite fashion was tantamount to the worst of crimes.

"It is much as usual. As I have noted, we have few guests here, but I am used to the effect I have upon others, for I am a frequent visitor to places which may or may not be expecting me. One learns to take such reactions in stride, however much one might wish it otherwise. I have no desire to cause discomfort to any."

"Oh, but you don't! At least, not to me. On the contrary, you have been kinder—more welcoming and more considerate—than any other I have encountered on my journeys."

"Even Jack Scrabbin or Hettie Toloch?" Theda asked with a low scratching sound I took to be laughter.

I shuddered at the reminder. "Hettie wished to make me a shroud."

"A high honor. She is a renowned seamstress. You may consider it a blessing."

"Where I come from such things are never discussed unless in the unwelcome presence of death itself."

More scratching noises and a certain shaking of its shoulders indicated Theda found this far more humorous than I would have expected. "You must forgive our little quirks, Avery Mothmere. We are much isolated here. Our customs will naturally appear out of the ordinary way to foreigners. But do get up now—you have soaked long enough. I would not wish you to catch a chill and undo all our good work."

The Dreadful Plunge

Such fears as circle round my brain, a maelstrom of oppressive thought, so familiar, so dear. Yet if you bade me pluck one down, describe it, I could not speak a word of its nebulous form. Not weight nor shape nor scent nor sound, such is the power they hold over my tongue.

    —excerpt from Memoirs of a Disgraced Magician

T HEDA WAS CORRECT THAT I was feeling more chilled than I had yet in this warm climate, so I was content to let myself be guided from the water and enfolded in a towel so large as to double as blanket if need be. My host gently patted me dry, then another round of bandaging followed, though fewer this time. I was pleased to observe that some of my lesser wounds were closing and even disappearing entirely. Theda's ointment must be very powerful to mend so quickly with no scarring. I considered again how fortunate I was to have fallen under the care of a talented healer after suffering such grievous injuries.

Too exhausted to face another trip downstairs, we agreed I would stay in bed while Theda fetched some evening sustenance for myself and Soot. When the door to my chamber reopened, however, it was the gilded child, Anchor, who stood there, carrying a tray of nourishing soup and more of the crusty, buttered bread with thin slices of a mild white cheese. The soup was lightly spiced and rich with root vegetables and green flakes of something like spinach. I had yet to see any meat served and pondered if vegetarianism was a part of the local traditions along with their unusual approach to funeral arrangements.

Soot was well-satisfied with whatever was in his bowl, finishing it quickly. He spent a few moments kneading one of the unused pillows on the bed with his white-booted paws before curling up in a comfortably round shape and closing his eyes. My own eyelids were heavy and I thought to follow suit. Anchor, who had lingered while I ate (though offering no conversation), reclaimed the tray and set it outside the door. Then, to my surprise, they came and sat on the end of the bed, cross-legged.

I marveled once more at their miraculous form—the gilt which fluttered and occasionally flew from their skin in wafting, papery pieces, like autumn leaves parting company with a branch. With their golden eyes, they reminded me of the carved, gilt figures adorning many a ceiling in one of the great palaces I had toured of late.

"Are you going to tell me another bedtime story?" I asked.

"If you wish. Or I can sing you a lullaby."

Intrigued by what counted as a lullaby in these parts (for music was a special passion of mine, and I had made many notes of the musical traditions of lands I had visited in my much-lamented lost journal), I opted for the cradle song as I reclined exhaustedly against the generous assortment of pillows.

If I tell you I've never heard anything so lovely as the tune the child sang. That it caused slow tears to leak from under my closed eyelids even while I chuckled softly in delight. That it sent a thrill through every cell of my body and riddled me with hope and despair in the same breath—even that will not convey the unearthly, exquisite beauty of their song. As the last clear notes fell, I drifted off to sleep, fully expecting to have nothing but the most pleasant of dreams after such a serenade, and for a time, I did.

I dreamt of a mermaid not unlike the figurehead on the ship, but lively and warm and made of flesh with scales which shone with as many colors as the infinite variety to be found in the sea. She held my hand tight as we dove beneath the waves. I knew at once I could breathe and be at home there. I knew my body was my own and yet not. It had been transformed in some indefinable way that made it alien, but not unpleasantly so. And I knew that this aquatic being meant me no harm.

Truly, there is nothing more tedious than listening to another person recall their dreams in any detail, so I will not linger upon the small adventures we had or what ocean creatures we met. Just assume all was well for a time. My first disturbance was the glimpse of red seaweed in the distance which waved long strands capped at the ends by pinching claws. Though I tried to protest, my mermaid companion pulled me along eagerly to this patch.

On closer inspection, I found there were bodies tangled within the waving forest. I recognized sailors from the ship, bloated and water-logged, including the Captain, who looked as angry in death as he had in life. His eyes suddenly opened wide, and he began to scream at me, "Your fault, your fault, your fault!" He struggled against the bonds which held him, as though anxious to free his arms so he might throttle me.

Breaking out of the mermaid's grasp, I backed away as quickly as I could. Another set of arms enfolded me from behind, and a most familiar voice whispered in my ear. Terrified, I broke away and turned to find Mitra, or the top half of her. As I watched, her lower half floated by and settled upon her head with legs pointing up like some grotesque hat.

I screamed, but the sound was much muffled by the water, which took advantage of my open mouth to pour within me, filling both stomach and lungs in an instant. Down I sank and down and down into the waiting arms of a giant cephalopodic monster such as I had heard many tales of from sailors but never seen. A cloud of black ink arose around me, and when I could see again, every part of my body but my face was covered in black, though it was not ink but a thin silk shroud which clung to me like a second skin.

Hettie Toloch and Theda and the gilded child appeared before me and as one, reached out and closed the final gap in the cloth, covering my face. I could not see or hear or speak. My entire being was terror, horror, panic, dread, alarm—all words insufficient to describe the sensation. Through the shroud, I could feel the bumps of small creatures and their grasping mouths. They pulled and prodded and ripped at me...

... and suddenly, I was awake, and the small mouth that prodded at me was Soot, licking the sweat from my fevered brow and bestowing small snuffling kisses upon my cheek. He seemed distressed, as if he had sensed my suffering and sought to put an end to it in any way he could.

With what relief did I sweep him into my arms, careless that the heat of his body and fur only added to my own unbearable burning. My covers were soaked through with sweat. I sprang from the bed, crossed over to a window and flung it wide. The air outside was scarcely cooler but was enough to provide a little relief. How long I stood there, stroking Soot and trying to soothe both him and myself while waiting for the reassurance of the first distant hint of dawn, I couldn't say. But I had never passed such a night before and hope never to again.

THE VAST LIBRARY

If you find your soul wearing thin, seek to preserve it by stowing it in a thrice-enchanted box carved with ancient runes and encrusted with mystic stones. You will also need seven locks bound with charms that can only be dissolved with the tears of a phoenix or the excrement of a wyvern. Once your soul is safely stored within, all should be well—so long as you do not misplace the box, as has happened on more than one notable occasion.

—excerpt from A Grimoire Malign

THE SUN CAME UP at last, as it always does if one is patient enough. Soot had grown tired of waiting in my arms and gone back to bed, but I still stood by the window, watching the shifting colors of dawn. I could see far from this high place. The patio, the garden, the lawn, the wall, the marsh, the forest. All in perfect arcs which were too planned and uniform to be natural.

I could also make out the roofs of the town buildings. What lay beyond? The beach where I had come ashore? Or were there other layers between us and the sea? So many questions, yet I remained shy of asking them of Theda or Anchor. But why? As a scientist, gathering facts and figures was second nature to me. Everywhere I traveled, I quizzed the local inhabitants on everything from marriage customs to their bathroom habits. Why should this be any different?

As I pondered, I performed a quick morning ablution, using a cloth and the cool water left in the basin to refresh my sweat-soaked skin. Upon investigation, I found another set of clothing similar to the first had been left in the wardrobe, but these were of a dusky grey color rather than white. I had just finished donning them when the door opened to reveal Anchor with another tray of food. They set it upon the bed, wordlessly, before leaving quickly again after gracing me with a deep bow.

Smiling to myself at this charming formality, I wolfed down the porridge, honey, and fruit, eager to get on with my day and determined to find out more about this place and my extraordinary hosts. As usual, a small dish was included for Soot, who ate as eagerly as I. When we were finished, I thought it only right to return the tray to the kitchen to save trouble. I was halfway down the stairs before realizing I had no idea where the food we'd enjoyed since our arrival was produced.

It being the only other room I was acquainted with, I went first to the large parlor on the ground floor, but neither Theda nor the child were there. Growing weary of carrying the heavy tray as I was not yet back to my full strength, I set it down upon the card table.

Gathering my courage, I climbed to the next floor, knocking first, then opening the wooden door I found there. With the greatest amazement and pleasure, I walked into an extensive library. Rich mahogany shelving curved right around the walls of the room from floor to ceiling, with a rolling ladder providing access to the higher shelves. Shorter, free-standing shelving formed circles within circles within the space, and in the center was a pair of comfortable, black-velvet wing-backed chairs with matching footstools.

There are few things which thrill me more than a well-stocked library, and this was one of the most impressive I'd seen outside of the grand municipal libraries in the largest of cities. Hoping I was not trespassing too much upon the goodwill of my hosts, I ventured in, scanning the shelves in growing amazement.

There were books here in every major language and untold obscure ones. They were organized in such a way that I was able to quickly find the sections with the three languages I spoke and read most fluently. The subject matter varied widely from lurid and low-brow novels to highly-scientific treatises on extraordinarily arcane topics.

I was not surprised to note a large section of occult tomes locked away behind glass. Investigations into the mysteries of the supernatural had been increasingly popular in the past decade or so. I approved that some security measures had been taken (for such books can be extremely dangerous if they fall into the wrong hands) while lamenting I could not get a closer look at the titles and content.

Tempted beyond measure, I couldn't help but pull a few books from other shelves and settle down in the inviting reading area to peruse them. They were exquisitely bound in rich tight-woven cloth with unique gilded designs upon the spines and covers. The golden decoration reminded me of the glowing skin of the child. I wondered if they were special editions, or if Theda or Anchor had a talent for bookbinding, as this was a hobby I much enjoyed.

"I see you have found your way to the library." Theda loomed over my shoulder suddenly, its iron-grey hair sweeping forward to brush my cheek.

Startled, I jumped to my feet, hiding the book in my hand behind my back as though I had been caught out doing something naughty.

"Be at ease, Avery Mothmere. Readers are welcome here, for what use is a book without someone to peruse its pages? I often feel sorry for them. They wait patiently upon their shelves, each hopeful today is the day they will be chosen. Who are the fortunate ones today?"

I showed it my handful, and it took each in turn most reverently, caressing the spines with gloved hands as if rediscovering old friends before handing them back to me.

"You have eclectic tastes. I will be interested to hear your opinion so I may compare it to my own."

"You've read these?"

"They are in my library, so naturally I have."

"But surely you've not read all of these books," I said, half-jokingly, for it was obvious that even if one did nothing else for the rest of one's life and was able to comprehend the wide array of languages represented upon the shelves, no one would be able to read even a modest portion of such a vast collection.

"Yes, all—and most more than once. I have had to pass many lonely hours. Do you admire the bindings? Anchor has rebound each one with a special design to suit the content. They have also known loneliness and the burden of countless hours to fill. Have you known loneliness, Avery Mothmere?"

THE AMATEUR BOOKBINDER

If they knew the end date, they could conserve their energy, harness hope for better days. But time is only a notebook of empty pages, unlined, recycled from days gone by. A memoir both poignant and humdrum unspools therein, written with a quill of steel and the bitter ink of unshed tears.

    –excerpt from The Chronicles of Disintegration

I SCARCELY KNEW HOW to respond to these extraordinary statements, much less the question that followed. Looking around at what must be thousands, if not tens of thousands of volumes or more—to have read so many books, or even rebound them all, were absurd statements. Yet Theda appeared to be serious, though of course it was difficult to judge as its expression never resolved into one which could be easily interpreted.

My eye was caught by the occult books trapped behind glass, and for the first time, I seriously considered whether I myself was caught up in a supernatural experience. Please do feel free to laugh at me. I laugh at myself thinking how dense I must seem or how naively willing to accept so many weird occurrences without wondering such before. My only defense must be that I was so shocked by the shipwreck, the sudden loss of my former comrades, and my ordeal on the beach that my usually agile mind was temporarily muddled.

I had read accounts of other worlds—slips in time and place, cracks which open in the stuff of the universe and allow one to travel onto planes that need not follow the rules or logic of our own. Though I'd previously dismissed these ideas as little better than fairy tales, there were too many bizarre things about this place which could not be easily explained away as simple differences in culture and custom.

That this revelation should come to me in a library was most natural as there was nowhere I was more at home and sensible than among books. And I knew what was involved and how many hours went into either reading or binding one. Doing some quick estimations and figures in my head, it was evident no normal lifespan would be sufficient to have accomplished such feats as Theda claimed, especially when one considered a person must sleep and eat and carry out other duties as well.

Though when I thought on it, I had never witnessed Theda or Anchor eat, nor did I possess any proof they slept. They were both most unusual in form—perhaps they were unusual in habit also and thus had more time on their hands than the rest of us. The more I sifted through these facts in my mind, the more I accepted there was something truly otherworldly about this place. Either that... or I was going completely mad.

I realized that Theda was waiting politely for some answer to its query while I stood open-mouthed, both much struck and distracted by my own startling train of thought.

"Books are... certainly... they are certainly... that is, they have been my friends..." I stammered. "That is, one is never truly alone when one has a book. To share the thoughts of its author and add your own is like a conversation of sorts, isn't it? And these bindings—they are some of the finest specimens of the art I have ever seen. Far more skillfully done than my poor talents would allow."

A musical voice piped up behind my back. "Do you practice the craft?"

It was Anchor, who had somehow entered the library without my noticing. (Though given my state of mind, I might not have noticed if a herd of rampaging elephants had passed by.)

Attempting to pull myself together, I answered. "I've dabbled. I enjoy making my own journals when I'm at home and have the time. I bound one specially for this voyage, but I'm afraid it must be at the bottom of the ocean."

"Come along! Come along!" The child grabbed my hand and pulled me after them. Their touch was warm and papery but somehow comforting, and their enthusiasm was so infectious, I found my spirits buoyed, regardless of my newfound fears as to what state of mind or place I found myself.

We climbed the stairs nearly to the top again, stopping on the floor beneath my own. Here I discovered a cozy but fully-stocked and organized studio. Iron book presses, giant shears, stacks of bookboard, rolls of cloth, and the indefinable scent of such a place: a mixture of glue and dust, sweat and mold. The dry burning smell of old paper and the sweet intoxication of performing tasks as familiar as they are satisfying.

"How fantastic!" I cried, unable to resist running to one of the workbenches which lined the circular walls and riffling through the familiar tools there.

The child seemed as excited as I. "You must make another journal, to replace what you have lost!"

From a shallow map drawer, they pulled a stack of creamy paper, the perfect weight and texture for the purpose. They busied themselves cutting the sheets to an appropriate size while I folded signatures in preparation for sewing.

With what joy did I take up needle and thread and begin the process of creating a text block thick enough for many notes but thin enough to be easily portable. I used a favorite sewing pattern and was absurdly pleased when Anchor praised my choice. What a delightful way to pass an hour or two, creating a useful object where before were only loose sheets of paper.

Then, oh so carefully putting it into the press, making sure everything is lined up exactly right before applying glue and linen to the spine to protect the sewing and ensure the book would lie open in a smooth arc when in use. Now we must wait for the glue to dry.

I passed the time by reading a book brought up from the library, a naturalist's account of their observations of creatures in the wild. How pleasant it was to sit there among the tools and equipment of the bookbinding trade while reading a book which had itself been beautifully bound. I felt more at home in those moments than in any others I'd experienced since landing on these strange shores.

Once the glue on the spine was set, it was time to cut board and cloth for the cover and choose some decorative endpapers. I picked a red wine buckram cloth, strong but with a fine, tight weave pleasant to touch. A wine- and gold-marbled paper would serve for inside the covers. The familiar measurements and movements came back to me, and I was filled with a confidence which was rare—for there are many small missteps one can make in the process which can lead to ruin.

This binding came out perfectly, however, if you will allow me to boast (for such was not always the case with my efforts). Then it was back into the press to set the hinges and make sure the cover boards did not warp or bend during the drying time.

"A noble effort," said Anchor approvingly. "You are the first I have met who revered the art as much as I. As reward, I will gild the cover for you if you wish, with whatever subject you desire."

I recognized at once this was a great honor, for the embellishments on the bindings in the library far surpassed in beauty and skill any I had ever seen. And I knew precisely what I wished for decoration.

"Will you draw me a map of this place?"

The Tentative Enquiry

I watched as a grey wolf nosed aside a bumblebee to discover an owl no larger than a grain of wheat perched upon the petal of a golden lily. They communed for hours on many subjects: wisdom, compassion, the meaning of life and of death. But never once did the wolf ask why the owl was so small, for some matters are simply none of our business.

—excerpt from A Naturalist's Observations of an Oft-Forgotten World

THE CHILD LAUGHED AND clapped their hands. "A map is a fitting motif, for I think you will have much to record of your experiences here before you depart. Leave it to me."

They tucked their hand confidingly into the crook of my arm and led me downstairs and out onto the patio. Another feast had been set up there on the wrought-iron table. This time there was a variety of cheese and condiments, pickles and thinly sliced roasted vegetables along with a delicate and frilly lettuce. Thick slices of a dark-hued bread indicated I was to construct a sandwich to my own taste, which I did readily, having worked up an appetite from the morning's unexpected but rewarding labor.

"Won't you join me?" I asked Anchor as they stood watching my choices with interest.

"Not for me such pleasures," they replied. I could not help but think it a perfect opportunity to inquire more into the nature of their life and of their very being, but again I was struck by an uncommon reluctance to what I could only think of as prying.

Giving myself a stern internal talking to, I ventured a mild query at last. "Is it not to your taste?"

"That matters not, as long as it is to yours." With this enigmatic utterance, the child turned and wandered away into the chaotic garden. There, they danced freely with the insects which buzzed so industriously, stopping often to bend over and inhale the varied scents of the flowers. Perhaps they whispered the secrets they would not share with me to the blooms.

It scarcely was polite or dignified to chase after them, sandwich in hand, to interrupt their pleasure and interrogate further. I wondered whether Anchor and Theda meant to be mysterious as a means to obfuscate or even protect me from some truth they thought best to hide, or if it was simply in their nature to express themselves in ways that were obscure to more mundane beings such as myself.

All of this pondering and doubt had left me on the verge of a headache. I refilled my glass with the cool lemonade which accompanied lunch and sipped it slowly while closing my eyes against the bright sun and heat. I concentrated on the gentle relief of the refreshing breeze which swirled around the walls of the tower and rustled the plants of the garden. The drone of insects, the frequent chirps and chattering of songbirds, and now and again, the high clear call of some hawk-like avian that I pictured soaring far above our heads, making ever-widening circles which mimicked the circular landscape below.

I was torn between wanting answers to my rapidly increasing store of questions and simply relaxing and enjoying what, for all I knew, was a unique experience among humankind. I itched to get my hands on the completed journal. Writing and sketching the things I'd seen would help clear space in my mind for calmer and more orderly thoughts.

It may surprise you to learn I am by nature a fearful and anxious person. You will think it impossible I would have undertaken so many journeys to unfamiliar places under such an impediment, but I had determined from a young age that I would not let my fears rule my existence. I had confronted and conquered many obstacles during my travels, but none, I must admit, so odd as my present predicament.

Theda reappeared at this moment, gathering the plates onto a tray for removal. Determined to speak of my own plight, even if I was too timid to quiz my hosts closely about themselves, I asked if it would join me and talk a while. It made a motion I took to be a nod, disappearing briefly with the tray and reappearing with a second chair which it placed beside my own, turning its face toward me while folding its gloved hands upon the lap where pooled the abundant hair.

"What is to become of me?" I asked. "Do you send and receive mail here? I'm without funds or supplies and would like to write to my family to let them know I am safe and see if they can send me what I need to continue on my way."

"We do not communicate often with the outside world, but you needn't worry. You may stay as long as you like."

"You are generous, but I must leave some time. It would be rude to infringe upon your hospitality indefinitely. What modes of transportation are available? Is there a port along the oceanfront? I might be able to earn passage on a ship through work as a member of the crew when I have more fully recovered my strength—if they will accept the help of one such as I that is."

"There is a craft which crosses the waters regularly. The fare is low by nature of the limited and rude accommodations it offers, but I would not be in a hurry to depart. Once you leave this place, you will not return. Why not stay and make such observations as you can? It is an opportunity few are granted."

"I would like to explore the countryside and town more, but it pains me to have no money to give you in recompense for room and board or to purchase any little necessities from the shops."

"As to necessities, we can provide what you need. As to recompense, we need none. As to money, it holds little sway here. Most merchants will gladly share their wares with you for no return other than a story they have never heard or a song which has never been sung within these borders. Novelty is most valued here."

This was news indeed. I had visited many cultures where bartering of goods and services was common, but none in which a simple story or song was so valued. I remembered how struck Jack Scrabbin had been with my tale. If very few outsiders visited these shores, any new face and tales of the wider world could be exciting enough to pass for a kind of currency, I supposed.

"You must count me rich then," I said with a laugh. "For I have countless reports of my travels and songs I've picked up from many lands."

"Then you will be as welcome in town as you are here. It is late in the day for such a visit, but tomorrow, go and visit as many shops as you like. And if you grow tired of such, venture beyond the town."

"Beyond the town? What is beyond the town? The beach where I was found? The ocean? Is it safe to venture there? Are there other dangers?"

"Nothing can truly harm you while you are within my domain. Go where you like but show respect to all you encounter. They each have their part to play and their own stories to tell, and none are more or less precious than your own."

THE DECK ARCANE

I can feel every tendon, every bone beneath my stretched-too-thin skin, and run fingers over the damask-patterned heart of me, so beautiful and raw beneath my touch. At eventide, at eventide, I chant to myself. What will happen then? I do not know and fervently hope I will never find out.

    –excerpt from Memoirs of a Disgraced Magician

I DECIDED TO FOLLOW Theda's advice of waiting until morning to make a return visit to the town. Though healing unnaturally swiftly, I was still easily exhausted, and the morning's exertions in the bookbinding studio had left me more worn than I liked to admit. I brought a selection of books from the library up to my room and delved into one or another in between napping on the bed with Soot nestled close, his soft, quiet puffs of breath a comforting accompaniment to either activity.

The books I had picked at random, being in languages of which I had enough fluency not to have to struggle to follow them. Besides the naturalist's diary, there was a somewhat dreary annal of a far-flung country whose history seemed to consist of nothing but disasters of one kind or another—I made a mental note never to travel there. A memoir written by a lowly conjurer and sometime fraud was hardly more uplifting. And as to the grimoire Theda allowed me to take from the locked cabinet? I was too afraid to open it just then—it glared balefully at me and hummed with a malignity which suited the title imprinted upon the spine in the child's lovely gilding.

Dissatisfied with my choices, I might have returned to the library to look for lighter fare if I weren't so comfortable. As it was, my deficit of restful slumber from the night before meant I was fighting sleep every few pages regardless of the content. Giving in more often than not, I passed the afternoon in a kind of daze of disjointed sentences and images that swirled together into fevered dreams, leaving me little more rested than if I'd never lain down at all.

Have you ever been caught in a cycle of dreams within dreams? Positive that you were now wide awake, only to discover you're still dreaming? To wake and wake and yet sleep. It's a terrible feeling, one which left me restless and panicked when I woke a final time and jumped from the bed, kneeling to feel the cool stone floor and the tangled bedcover and Soot's fluffy head as he peered over the edge of the mattress at me. To reassure myself by this tangible evidence that I had finally escaped the loop which sought to keep me trapped in a nightmare.

I got up and staggered to the basin, pleased to see it had been refilled with clean water. I wondered idly when such niceties were carried out and if all by Theda or the child. It was surprising such an establishment would have no maids or housekeeper to assist in cleaning and cooking and the other thousand little chores that went into running an establishment of this size, but no more puzzling than anything else I had noticed.

When I was more myself again, I wandered back down the staircase, speculating as to what was behind the door on each of the floors. My bedchamber up top and the binding studio below were two. The ground floor parlor and the library above it made four. That left nine floors yet unexplored. Assuming Theda and Anchor each had a floor for their own personal use (did they have need of such mundane spaces?), there would be seven left. Presumably a kitchen of some sort must exist to produce the food I had consumed, but I could scarcely speculate on what other uses they might have for all this space.

I pictured the rooms at home and smiled to think of my hosts in the games room, leaning over the billiards table, taking aim with stick in hand. Our conservatory was filled with exotic plants that Mother wrote away for and nurtured (often with more care and attention than ourselves). There was the ballroom and grand dining hall. Father's study, where he kept his own collection of books separate from the main library. The front and back parlors. The music room. So many specialized and ultimately wasted spaces, for we rarely used the more formal areas. It was hard to imagine my stately hosts needing rooms dedicated to these relatively frivolous activities.

But when I arrived at the ground floor of the tower, I discovered to my surprise that Theda and the child were involved in something as seemingly inconsequential as a card game. Both were seated at the round mahogany table, and Theda was dealing the cards with surprising dexterity given the limitations of handling thin paper stock with gloves on. I approached close enough to watch, curious whether I would recognize the game, but not so close as to disturb them.

The deck they were using was beautiful, but not at all the standard French-suited, fifty-two-card set I was familiar with. Instead, the oversized cards were decorated with intricate scenes painted in rich colors which reminded me of tarot sets I had seen before. There were figures on the flip side of each of the cards—human, I thought, though it was hard to make out details at distance.

The cards were dealt so quickly and efficiently, it was difficult for my eye to follow, but Theda seemed to be creating a clockwise pattern with piles at north, south, east, and west, then a pile along the circle in between each of these points, and one central pile as well. When the deck of cards in front of Theda was completely dealt, the two players took turns picking up a card and turning it over. Though I watched closely, I could discern no pattern or purpose to their moves.

Sometimes, one of them would shake their head and move a card after their opponent played it, as though correcting some mistake. Occasionally, they stopped to discuss something in low voices, with one or the other of them arguing passionately some point that their opponent seemed to disapprove or even regret.

I watched for some time, gradually drawing nearer to the table in my interest, but could not discern whether either player was gaining an advantage over the other, for the number of cards and general distribution stayed much the same. How long they might have continued, I was not to discover as Theda suddenly swept the cards together, straightening and reconstituting them into a single undealt deck.

"Forgive us, Avery Mothmere," it said. "We often become so engrossed in this task that all other considerations are neglected."

Task was an odd word choice for what was surely a game of some sort but, feeling I had unwittingly interrupted them (and reminded that having an uninvited guest when you were not used to company was quite an imposition), I once again hesitated to inquire further despite my burning curiosity. I suppose you are lambasting my passivity, but I can only say that you were not there and have never experienced the eerie and oppressive atmosphere which lay over that place and time. Perhaps you think you would have been braver.

I sincerely hope you never have the opportunity to find out if that is true.

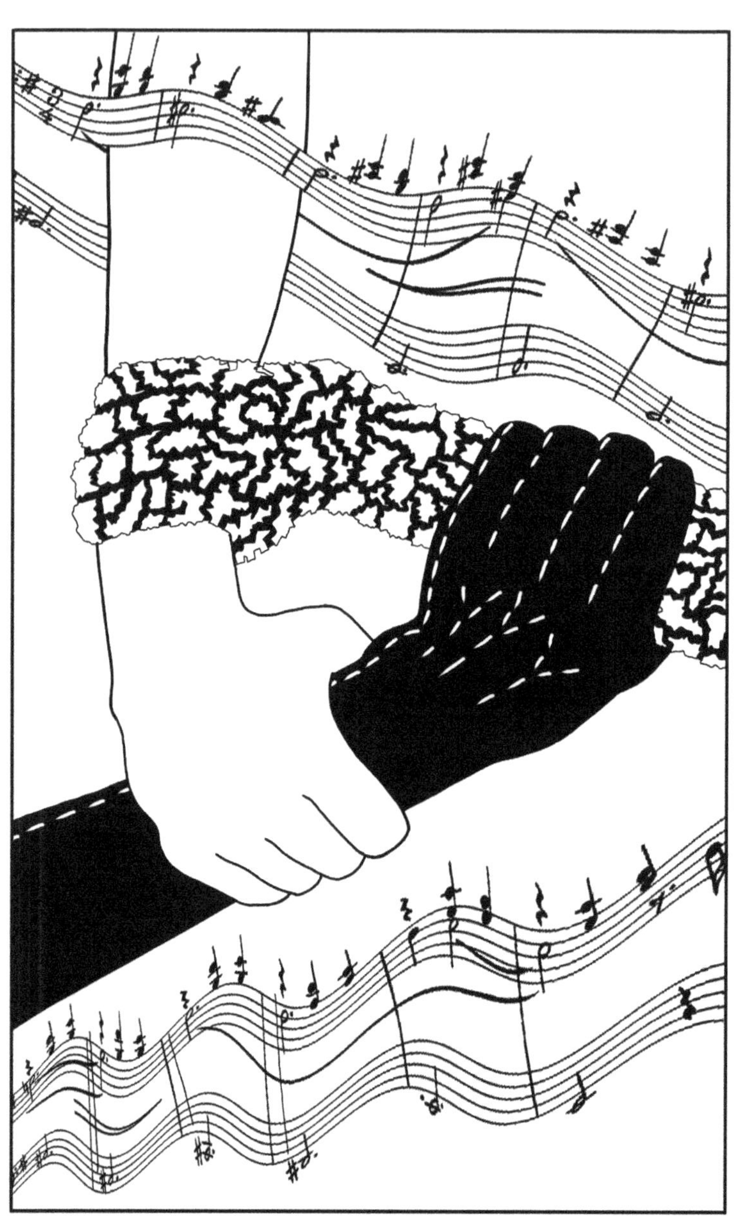

The Plaintive Waltz

It is well-known that phantoms go visiting at night. If once you encourage them, they will come more and more often, beating at the door, rattling the windows, prying at the shutters, for they are most persistent and obstinate callers. The following recipe is useful for mending any gaps in your protection spells.

—excerpt from A Grimoire Malign

MY APOLOGIES FOR DISRUPTING their unusual activity were quickly though kindly dismissed. I was encouraged to take my place at the table while Theda disappeared with the deck. I was disappointed, as I would have relished the opportunity to examine it more closely, but Anchor distracted me by drawing from me how I'd spent my afternoon. I described the books I had been skimming, making light of their rather dour and disturbing content, but somehow, before I knew it, was also confessing my troubled dreams, both during my nap and the night before.

"They are not real," the child remarked. "Light and shadow only."

"Yes, of course," I agreed, "though at the time, they can be as real and frightening as any experience one has while awake, so they do have a sort of reality, don't you think?"

"It depends on how you define the word."

"Things that are real are tangible, I suppose. Like this table that I can feel beneath my hands and the chair which is solid and supports me."

"But, in a dream, might you not also have these sensations?"

"Yes, the pressure of the water against my skin felt real and the mermaid's hands in mine also."

"Then how do you know you are not dreaming even now?"

"Things would seem more strange, surreal in a dream."

"And do you find nothing here strange or surreal?"

Staring into the gilded child's golden eyes as they studied me like I was a mildly interesting natural history specimen pinned helplessly to a board, I was painfully conscious of my otherness and even my wrongness in this place. I didn't belong here and had stumbled across it by the merest chance. I was sure it appeared on no map and was confident if I ever once left, as Theda had warned, I would never find my way back here again.

For all their peculiarity, I'd never really been afraid of Anchor or Theda, but now, as I felt the child watching and waiting for my answer, I sensed a kind of—malevolence is too strong a word, but a separation, as if we existed on such different planes that I was no more to my hosts than a beautiful butterfly was to me. Something to be admired briefly but having no influence or meaning beyond a passing shared moment in time and space.

"Do not annoy our guest with your philosophy, Anchor," Theda said, returning with a tray. "You must forgive them. They enjoy teasing but have so few opportunities."

I busied myself with receiving and rearranging the dishes Theda handed me, an evening meal of clear broth, more roasted vegetables over a bed of fragrant rice, and small dumpling-like pastries full of a pleasantly spicy filling which swiftly set me to perspiring. Having taken advantage of this pause to gather my thoughts, I ventured a reply.

"It is an interesting topic. Reality, that is. Many learned minds, both philosophers and scientists have debated these same questions. I must confess to finding it unsettling. I prefer to think that I understand when I'm awake and when I'm dreaming. When the things around me truly exist and when they are a mirage or hallucination. I've met some who saw things the rest of us did not and pitied them, for if one cannot trust one's own mind and thoughts, then the world becomes a place of chaos and disorder."

"And chaos and disorder are to be abhorred," said Theda. "On this we agree. I have many duties and responsibilities. To perform one of my tasks too late or forget it entirely would be unforgiveable. Therefore, a faultless system of organization is a necessity."

"Unforgiveable? Can that be true? Surely there are few tasks so important that they cannot be postponed or undertaken by another?"

"My tasks are my own and no other's."

"It sounds a heavy burden," I said, touched by some tone in Theda's voice which indicated it was not entirely as sanguine about its duties as it would like to portray.

"Having never experienced any other existence, I have nothing to compare it to. We all have a part to play, Avery Mothmere. Do not accept any burdens other than your own."

I bent my head in acknowledgement of this advice and turned my attention back to my meal. Theda and the child arose as if of one accord. Hand-in-hand, they proceeded to the center of the room and began a curiously elegant dance as a tune sprang up around us. I craned my neck to try to find the source of the melody, but there was no obvious phonograph or other musical device I could see.

It was a waltz in the traditional three-quarter time and in a minor key both melancholy and divine. Food forgotten, I stood up and joined them as they made way for me. Grasping one gloved hand and one dry, papery one, we circled round, dipping and diving in time to the music while Soot wove in and out effortlessly around our ankles, somehow managing to never trip us. Anchor and Theda both sang along, echoing the haunting air wordlessly. I followed suit, though so shyly (being self-conscious of my limited vocal abilities) that I doubt I added much to the choir.

When the song ended, I bade them goodnight immediately and ascended the stairs, for I was so transported by the magic of the music and the dance that any further activities or conversation were superfluous and even undesirable. Soot ran ahead of me, eager to rejoin the comfort of his pillow upon the bed.

Upon reaching my room, I lay down again, humming, trying to catch and hold the tune while once more lamenting the lack of a diary where I might have recorded the procession of notes while it was fresh in my mind. I could not regret the opportunity to have a journal with a binding decorated by an artist so skilled as Anchor, however, so I resolved to wait in patience until they were done with their part of the process.

And so to sleep once more and once more to dream (or was it a dream within a dream?) There were things within these visions meant to frighten me, images of mindless evil and calculating coldness, of pain and torture and losses beyond bearing. But through it all, a waltz of infinite sadness and infinite beauty echoed, bringing me such comfort that I knew I was no longer alone inside my nightmare.

THE RUEFUL DAY

The dead call in the night with words meant to chill the bones: I am underneath the sycamore tree. You know the one. Come find me, come find me. It's lonely here with none but the crows for company. I'm chilled from the winter rains and fear soon snow will fall and it will be too late—hidden I'll be. Come find me, come find me and keep me company.

   —excerpt from The Chronicles of Disintegration

THE NEXT MORNING FOUND me the most refreshed I'd been since before my ordeal on *The Serendipity* began. Theda brought me breakfast in bed and tended to my wounds. All but a few were closed. In many places, no sign at all remained of the countless small bites of me that the crabs had taken. A quick wash and change of clothes (these even greyer in hue than the day before) and I was ready.

Eager to return to exploration after my day in the tower, I set out again to town with Soot, confidently retracing the path we'd taken before. The only challenging part was navigating the forest, for there was no clear path and one had perforce to wind among the trees. Afraid we would once again lose ourselves there, it was with intense relief that I spied the grey raven, who guided us safely to the edge of its home before disappearing back among the trees in an explosion of wing and feather.

The wheat field rustled in a brisk breeze, creating undulating patterns that reminded me of watching the unceasing movement of the ocean from the deck of a ship. I recalled that Theda had indicated there was a boat which serviced this land. I would have to investigate from where it departed and what fare I would have to raise, for even if it was modest, I'd not a penny to my name. I remembered also that Theda had advised exploring beyond the town, and I will admit to a burning curiosity as to what other layers there might be to the ever-widening circles within circles I had seen so far.

We crossed over the field and entered the town again, only to find it much less busy than on our previous visit. I had lost any sense of time and the passage of days. Was it Sunday? Did they have Sundays here? And were they the quiet days of worship and reflection common back home? I had no notion of what religion, if any, was practiced locally. Such knowledge might have given some indication as to whether this society also celebrated a day of rest.

The shops were closed, and the few people we saw rushed about like they were late for some event. I wandered as far as Hettie's turquoise door, wondering whether she was truly working on my shroud while shrinking from finding out. As I dithered, the door opened, and that selfsame person came bustling down the steps and took me by the arm.

"You've returned! How delightful, but I've no time to show you my progress, sweetie. I'm afraid I'm late as usual, but it is a lucky thing, for I can show you the way."

So saying, she pulled me along the sidewalk and guided me through a narrow alleyway I'd missed on my previous explorations. We emerged into an open space behind the town buildings. A large stone structure there with a tall spire and belfry would seem to indicate a church or other religious building, though it had none of the usual symbols I would associate with religions I had encountered.

A great bell began to ring out with low, bellowing booms which sent a thrum through the very earth beneath our feet. From the church (as I will refer to it for lack of a better term), a crowd of such size issued that I was perplexed as to how they had fit within its walls.

The people fanned out and busied themselves among a vast graveyard of tombstones which were each alike in size and shape. I stepped forward to examine those closest. Each marker had a traditional slab-like shape with rounded top. Each one also had a unique design carved into it—though curiously, no name or dates or any epigraphs as you might expect.

To give some idea of the artwork, one had a fierce owl in flight, wings curved and flexed in such a way as to show off the immensely detailed feather pattern. Its talons protruded from the stone giving the impression it was about to break free of its granite bonds and take off into the air. Another had a horse's bridle, with long reins that looped and twisted back and forth upon themselves like a bucket full of squirming eels. A third had a reaper's sickle, carving a path through a field of intricately rendered wheat not unlike the field between forest and town.

The cemetery itself stretched a good thirty to forty graves deep (if you can imagine thirty to forty corpses laid head to foot in perfectly straight lines radiating away from you). I was not surprised to see it also extended in an arc as far as I could see in either direction. Yet another circle thus was added to the pattern of this place (though it was daunting to think of what a multitude of the dearly departed such a space would encompass). I couldn't exactly make out what was on the far side of the graves and determined to make my way thence as soon as possible.

Hettie had marched away from me as though on a mission, and Soot and I followed to see what she was doing.

"We tend the dead," she said, as we approached. "It is our calling."

Like the other townspeople around us, she was leaving items upon the gravestones—an offering, perhaps? She stopped at each of the markers I've described, pulling from the small wicker basket she carried an object which related in some way to the image.

For the owl, she left a felted mouse, sewn with so much skill that it looked entirely realistic except for the glassy jeweled eyes. For the reins and bridle, she left an iron horseshoe, twined round with pink ribbon. For the sickle and wheat, she left a pair of bone dice, carefully placing them so the "ones" were facing upward, forming what I had heard referred to as snake eyes by those who indulge in the gambling arts.

This ritual continued for all of the stones in a single row. Each of the other rows had their own dedicated caretakers leaving similar presents. A charming custom, I thought—gifts for the dead as we might have left cut flowers at home, but flowers wilt. These were less transient gifts.

"How often do you perform this service?" I asked Hettie, thinking it was only on special holidays a few times a year.

"You will find us here every Ruesday."

"Tuesday?" I asked, thinking I had misheard.

"No, sweetie, wouldn't that be a chore!" she answered, chortling. "Only on Ruesday, which is a rare occurrence, at least here. Does it come around more frequently where you're from?"

"We don't have such a day that I'm aware of."

"What a shame! But how do you know when to tend to the dead?"

"Do the dead need much care? After all, they are... well... dead."

I became suddenly aware we had attracted a small crowd. Their eyes were focused upon me, and I couldn't help thinking it was in a most disapproving manner. Had I committed some social gaffe? These people seemed to have unusual, but firmly-held ideas centered on death and dying (if preparing your shroud in advance and leaving gifts in such an organized fashion for the dead were any indication).

Chilled, I waited, heart beating fiercely, sure I was about to receive a metaphorical or even literal lashing from an unfriendly crowd and wishing very much that I had held my tongue.

The Dreadful Thought

I am naught but a rickety man, rain-washed and slick with the brackish grot of memory. I careen through hollow streets, desperate to find another, but there is only me. I catch glimpses from the corner of my eye—they mean to make a fool of me, but they are too late. Since the end of days, I can no longer tell reality from visions. Am I awake or dreaming? Sahar used to tell me true, but Sahar is lost to us now.

—excerpt from Memoirs of a Disgraced Magician

ROARS OF MERRIMENT BROKE out all around me, and I was nearly knocked over under the buffeting not of angry blows, but hearty and good-natured slaps on the back.

"That were a good one, it was!"

"A prankster, aye?"

"Wait until I tell Ma. She do enjoy a good jest!"

These were a few of the comments I caught, and while I was relieved they were neither offended nor angry, I couldn't help but notice that no one offered any further explanation of either the Ruesday tradition or the local attitudes toward the dearly departed. Having already skated by a possibly ugly situation and with heart pounding from what felt like a narrow escape, I decided to hold my tongue and observe, smiling and laughing with the townspeople like I was in on the joke.

As Hettie bustled along her row, I took the opportunity to wander farther afield, making note of the offerings of others. The variety and quality were astounding, as it became obvious most of the gifts were hand-made by artisans or hobbyists of varying skill and talent, but the sentiment behind the objects was clearly sincere and touching. It became a kind of game to decipher how each item related to the image on its stone. Some were obvious, like the mouse and horseshoe, while others were more obscure to me, like the pair of bone dice for the reaping stone.

I could only assume the objects and the images on the gravestones were memorials to either the departed's profession, interests, or personality—or in some cases, a combination of all three perhaps. It seemed extraordinary that the townspeople could remember who was buried in each plot, particularly without the aid of inscriptions. Yet they often stopped and spoke to the markers as though they were visiting with an old friend, sharing gossip or a memory in addition to the small tokens left behind. Though foreign to my experience, I couldn't help but think it was a charming custom and provided the mourners with the comfort of knowing that when their own time came, they also would not be forgotten.

I gradually worked my way toward the outer edge of the cemetery, curious as to what lay beyond. I had hopes I would catch a glimpse of the rocky cliffs and the beach below. I didn't hear the ocean, but surely it could not be too far away. Immense was my disappointment to discover past the last of the graves a stone wall so high that I could not see over it, nor could I see any gap or gateway through which to pass.

Returning to Hettie's side, I enquired as to the best way to surmount this obstacle.

"An opening appears when needed, sweetie. What would be the use of a door at any other time?" was all she replied, and though I persisted in asking questions (for I was tired of perfectly natural curiosity being turned aside with cryptic answers), she only hummed a jaunty tune and pretended not to hear me.

I'm not sure why this should be the moment above any other when I began to seriously doubt my sanity, but so it was. I thought back over the unlikely events that had piled one upon another over the past few days of my existence. I pondered the strange beings I'd met and their unusual customs. And most of all, I considered the architecture and landscape—the round stones so perfectly placed for every purpose, the circles within circles, and at the center of it, the looming tower of unique design.

Having traveled widely and visited many countries, I'd discovered that, while each had its own distinctive features, there were many more commonalities among cultures than differences, but this place was utterly without precedent, with far too many inexplicable features. Therefore, as Anchor had suggested, I was either trapped within a dream or had lost my grip on reality altogether. My mind had taken up residence in a world that it had constructed from random memories and snippets of the many books, both speculative and scientific, I had read.

If this was true, I wondered where my body really was at that moment. Was I still aboard *The Serendipity*, riding out the storm? This seemed logical since the first weird thing I remembered was the arrival of the unholy worms upon the deck. But wait—further back still, the wave that washed Mitra overboard, splitting her in two with improbable force. Was such even possible? Then there was the series of storms, the plague which had decimated the crew, the other misfortunes that the superstitious sailors were quick to attribute to our presence as passengers among them.

Sitting down with my back against the high wall to rest (or at least to rest my dream body), I tried to remember the last time life had felt normal. Mitra and I waiting at the little restaurant by the pier, our luggage piled up beside the table. We'd cleared our empty dishes to the side to make room for my diary. Sketching out the route I expected the ship to take, we speculated on how many days we might be at sea before our intended destination.

A scarlet and gold parrot flew over, landed on Mitra's hat, and set about soiling it. How we roared at the absurd event and exerted ourselves to soothe the harassed and embarrassed owner with assurances that there was no lasting harm done. He bought us both a drink and toasted our good health and safe journey.

There—that was the last good moment I remembered. Maybe the drinks were drugged, and I was lying in some back alley, dazed and dreaming, having been robbed and discarded by canny thieves. I'd wake up soon and Mitra would be beside me, similarly confused but eager to tell me of the things she'd dreamt.

Could I will myself awake? Though much of this dream had been interesting and even pleasant, it wasn't comfortable in the least to think I might be trapped. Then again, if I had gone mad, perhaps no awakening could be expected. There were few treatments for insanity, although I'd recently read a scientific abstract trumpeting new techniques with promising results. If I was mad, I hoped very much that I was an inmate in a more forward-thinking institution than the ones back home. Such places were notorious for their abuse of their unfortunate patients, who were often exploited and even displayed for the amusement of the idle rich. I shuddered to think I might be incarcerated in such a place without being aware of it.

Having finished his own exploration of the cemetery, Soot came over to sit upon my lap. Here was a link—my only link—between the before and the after. All evidence of my previous life had been washed away, but this one creature remained. I ran a hand over his silky fur, felt his rough tongue against my fingers, and observed the slight rise and fall of his breath. How warm and alive and very, very real he seemed. While it did not resolve my fears, the comfort I took in his small but reassuring presence at such a critical moment of emotional crisis is one I shall never forget.

The Merciless Parade

A species of vine creeps round their ankles and slinks up their arms, a green embrace which anchors the combatants to the ground. Their bodies feed the plants and the plants, in turn, prevent their spirits from being consumed by far worse enemies—a symbiotic relationship. They whisper verdant secrets to their victims. An utterance of sap-laced lies, but oh, how sweet! If only they didn't take far more than they gave.

    -excerpt from The Chronicles of Disintegration

WHAT WOULD YOU DO if you were as lost as I was at that moment, sitting with my back against a wall with no door, watching—mourners? supplicants? caretakers?—tending a perfect grid of graves, while you pondered whether or not you were mad? If you were me, you would determine to sharpen your scientific mind and open your senses to everything around you. If there was one skill I possessed, it was a talent for observation. Whether this place was real or not, I meant to learn everything I could about it and in so doing, hope to come to some conclusion about my own state of mind.

I strolled along the towering wall, brushing my fingers against the smooth stones, those flawless spheres which were integral to so many features in this place. No imperfections or openings marred the wall's surface, and the crest of it was well above my head, so there was no way to see what was beyond. I pictured myself finding a ladder and climbing to the top, wondering if any of the townspeople would intervene to prevent it. They seemed to be paying me little attention other than smiling and nodding in a friendly fashion if I happened to catch their eye.

No ladder being handily on offer in the cemetery, I thought to explore the church-like structure where the bell still rang out—a slow, sonorous sound. (If it was tolling a peal for each of the dead, it might be tolling after nightfall and beyond.) It occurred to me the church might have a storage room or basement where tools and equipment as mundane as a ladder might be found. And even if not, I was curious to see the inside of the building, discover if it did have a religious purpose, and if so, learn more about what god or gods were worshipped there.

As I neared, I saw the church was larger than I had estimated when at distance. It now seemed less improbable that the town's inhabitants had fit within its walls before filing out to tend to their grave duties. It was a simple four-sided structure with sloped roof atop which perched the four-sided belfry. As I had noticed from afar, a sharp spire rose to a point high above. Up close, it became clear this was a sculpture—a work of art—rather than a plain architectural feature.

The spire was formed by a lizard, twisting and curling in curious configurations until the very tip of its tail formed the uppermost point. Its body was covered in a chiseled geometric pattern meant to represent the scales of the reptile, and the creature had three heads descending above the belfry, each with an open mouth exposing a set of sharp fangs. I wondered if they served the same purpose as the gargoyles I'd seen mounted on stately monuments. There, the statues served as not only decoration but also performed the practical function of funneling rainwater.

This begged the question of whether it ever rained in this hot, dry climate. Surely it must or else the garden and lawn at the tower would be long dead—unless there was some irrigation system there I was unaware of. Perhaps they had the seasonal rainfall of many arid places, when a year's worth of moisture fell within the span of a few days or weeks. Survival was hard in such lands, and it was a testament to the inhabitants who lived there that they had the resilience and ingenuity to thrive under conditions so inhospitable to life.

The front doors of the church stood open, though no one was around. I ventured in. There was a single large room with benches—or pews—arranged in circles around a central seal set into the floor and carved of the same granite as the gravestones. The image on the seal was of a field of wheat not dissimilar to the one on the stone that Hettie had tended, but instead of a sickle, this wheat was being cut by a long-handled scythe such as I'd seen used in some of the less mechanically-advanced farming cultures I'd visited.

The inference was clear—wheat being cut down as we are cut down soon or late. I was not surprised to see such a common symbol of death here in this place which served as a hub for the largest gathering of the dead I'd ever seen. There was a mural along the walls, however, which was more curious and less easy to interpret. Painted in vivid blues and greens, garish reds and yellows, it depicted a series of creatures—beasts, monsters?—unlike any that I was aware of from the natural world.

Many-limbed and many-mouthed. Winged more often than not or blessed with fins and tails like a fish. And everywhere were eyes, too many eyes. I felt them watching me, and when I turned my head quickly, convinced I had seen movement, caught more than one of them blinking. No doubt a trick of the light from the sun which streamed through the open windows, playing games with the shadows. But that didn't explain the low hum, a subtle vibration as of many clawed and hoofed and webbed feet in motion, marching in an endless parade.

One of the creatures in particular fascinated me. It had a head like a ram with curling horns, a snake-like body covered with reddish-brown fur, and seven pairs of double-jointed arms or legs, each ending in suckered toes such as I had observed on a chameleon (which used these convenient appendages to cling and climb upon any surface without fear of falling).

Its mouth was a gaping, empty maw—a black void which stood out amongst the bright hues around it and sparkled here and there as if dusted with silvery mica. I lifted my hand to it, wanting to feel the texture of the surface under my fingers. As I rested my palm against the open mouth, a thousand needle-like teeth sprang out, piercing skin and bone. Shrieking, I attempted to pull away but was held fast to the wall as the monster's many ice-blue eyes blinked fiercely at me, some encrypted message or code I could not decipher, or so I fancied.

The other creatures came to life around us, roaring and howling and screeching in tones that easily drowned out my own protests. The whole procession began to march around the walls. Pinned as I was to the terrible ram-beast, I was forced to walk along with them, my palm dragging across the surface of the walls from corner to corner, on and on. How long a time this macabre and weird parade continued, I've never been able to reconstruct, but it seemed endless.

Finally, exhausted and clumsy, I stumbled once, twice... and I was down. I thought this might end the horror, but the relentless march went on, dragging me along the smooth-cobbled floor as I objected weakly, unable to make myself heard above the din. What agony as my arm was pulled from its proper place, the muscles stretching and tearing. I wished it would separate from my body entirely so at least I would be free.

My head, lolling helplessly, struck wall and floor more than once. My thoughts grew dim and confused. Never have I welcomed the absolute serenity and release of blessed oblivion with such grateful relief as I did in those final moments of uncompromising and undeserved cruelty.

Avery Mothmere

THE EMPTY PAGE

Outside my window, bees pester quince blossoms; a wild rabbit looks round and slyly steals blades of grass; squirrels hurtle across the fence, a tightrope chase; Lord Cardinal and his lady discover the puddle in the lowest spot of the yard, water flies, an impromptu bath. So much life goes on just outside my window—but I am on the inside.

—excerpt from A Naturalist's Observations of an Oft-Forgotten World

A SMALL TONGUE, ROUGH but tender, lapped at my nose. I awoke to the comforting sight of dear Soot, golden-eyes wide, black pupils thin slits, staring at me with what I chose to interpret as concern. Taking inventory, I soon discovered my offended arm was in a sling which kept it hugged close to my chest. My hand was wrapped up so tightly and comprehensively that I was unable to even see my fingers, much less move them. But any concerns I had around my injuries were superseded by my amazement to find I had somehow been transported back to the safety of my bedchamber in the tower.

I had only the vaguest memory of the torment at the church, though more and more of the hellish details returned to me over the next few hours as my brain rallied. I was far too exhausted to even consider getting up, content to await the return of either of my hosts as I pondered the morning's events. I noted it was dark outside and wondered how long I'd been unconscious.

How peculiar the passage of time was here. It was too easy to lose track of minutes, hours, days. So unlike my life before. I'd always kept a careful and precise record of each day's events, making plans and schedules to such a degree that I must have been exceedingly irritating to my travel companions in retrospect. As I was idly resting and thinking upon these topics, I noticed a beautifully decorated book lay beside me on the bed.

Recognizing the red wine-hued covering, I snatched it up eagerly. It was the blank journal I had made, but now the case was covered with delicate gold tooling. Spanning the spine and spilling over front and back was the central tower, interrupted by my name, Avery Mothmere, written out in an elegant script as though I was to be both title, subject, and author of the book.

On either side of the tower was a loose map of sorts, showing delicate vignettes of my experiences. Here, Soot and I shared Jack Scrabbin's pastry. There, Hettie Toloch and her ever-present basket stood among the rows of gravestones, smiling. The golden stag was embraced by the giant of the forest while the grey raven was shown, wings spread in flight. These images reminded me that while I had suffered through terrifying dangers, I'd also met with kindness, concern, and wondrous marvels.

I puzzled over a rowboat perched upon an empty shore, oars at the ready. Was this meant to be a lifeboat? A reference to the sunken vessel which had brought me close to this place before drowning? Or was it an oblique allusion to something yet to come—my departure. While Theda seemed in no hurry for me to leave, maybe the child did not share its complacency. Had they included this scene as a subtle visual impetus to remind me of my interrupted journey and encourage me to move on?

There were other, darker scenes. Anchor had drawn themselves standing at the top of the cliff—the moment they'd rescued me from being eaten alive. While grateful for their aid, I wasn't thrilled about having a constant reminder of the horror I had undergone on the beach. Nor was I happy to see immortalized in fine detail the writhing worms from the ship and even the monster from the church whose teeth had pierced my hand.

Though disappointed the child had decided to include such poignant and disturbing memories, I decided it would be churlish to complain when the gift was so special—for there is nothing more precious than someone sharing their creativity, skill, and effort with you. It is a gift which makes the giver vulnerable, exposed even, and so should be embraced fully and unreservedly. And perhaps it was beneficial to be reminded that in our lives, we must expect and accept sorrows alongside joy.

One omission puzzled me: Theda was nowhere represented. I still wasn't sure what its role was in this country. But the fact that others had spoken of the tower and its occupants with respect, if not outright awe, had made me wonder if it was the ruler of this land. The way it seemed to occupy itself with small domestic tasks made this notion puzzling, for my experience with those in high office was that they were above such trivialities.

Also, it had sworn I was under its protection as if it had the power to guarantee this. The attack in the church had exposed this promise as, at best, overly optimistic. Maybe it was not Theda who had absolute authority over this land but the child instead. I'd seen no evidence that Anchor concerned themselves with matters of the town or even much beyond the tower, so what had brought them to the cliff's edge the day I washed ashore—coincidence? Or did they have some system of watchers and signals which had alerted them to my presence?

Maybe someone had seen the ship foundering and summoned the child to provide assistance to any survivors, but it was strange none of the townspeople had gathered on the beach if that was the case. If they enjoyed novelty as much as reported, surely there is no experience so astonishing and engaging as the sudden appearance and subsequent shipwreck of a vessel not meant to sail so close to an uncharted shore.

Maybe and perhaps and what ifs... these words were becoming too frequent companions of late. I thought again of my fears that I was mad. That these wild events were simply playing out within my fevered brain. It was the simplest explanation to account for all of the contradictions and questions which roiled my thoughts.

I decided the best thing I could do would be to record everything that had happened to me so far. If I saw it laid out in black and white, I might perceive some logic or pattern that was eluding me. If only I had a pen or pencil.

As if in answer to my thought, Soot, who had been playing "catch my own tail" amongst the pillows, pounced and pulled out a black velvet pouch by the corded drawstring that held it closed. Presenting it like one of his rat trophies, he curled up and looked at me with satisfaction, very pleased with himself.

"Clever boy," I praised him absently, scratching his chin briefly as reward before turning my attention to the contents of the bag.

Fumbling a bit, as I was reduced to only one functional hand, I managed to draw out a simple four-sided bottle which contained a dark, thick liquid I took to be ink. There was also an elegant fountain pen of a most-advanced design. It was carved from some off-white material cool to the touch, though it was not marble or any other stone I was familiar with. Discovering the pen was already filled and ready, I grasped it (blessing the fates that my dominant hand was undamaged) and began to write.

How intimidating it is to mar the first pristine page in an empty journal, particularly as I was not fond of my handwriting. It was always sloppier and more imprecise than I liked, due to my haste to get my thoughts down before losing them. I'd often been told my script was indecipherable. However, if you're reading this now, then someone has managed to transcribe these poor notes into some coherent form and make them available for your perusal, and I hope, enjoyment.

Unless you're reading this selfsame volume I hold now in my hand... in which case, who are you and how did you come by it?

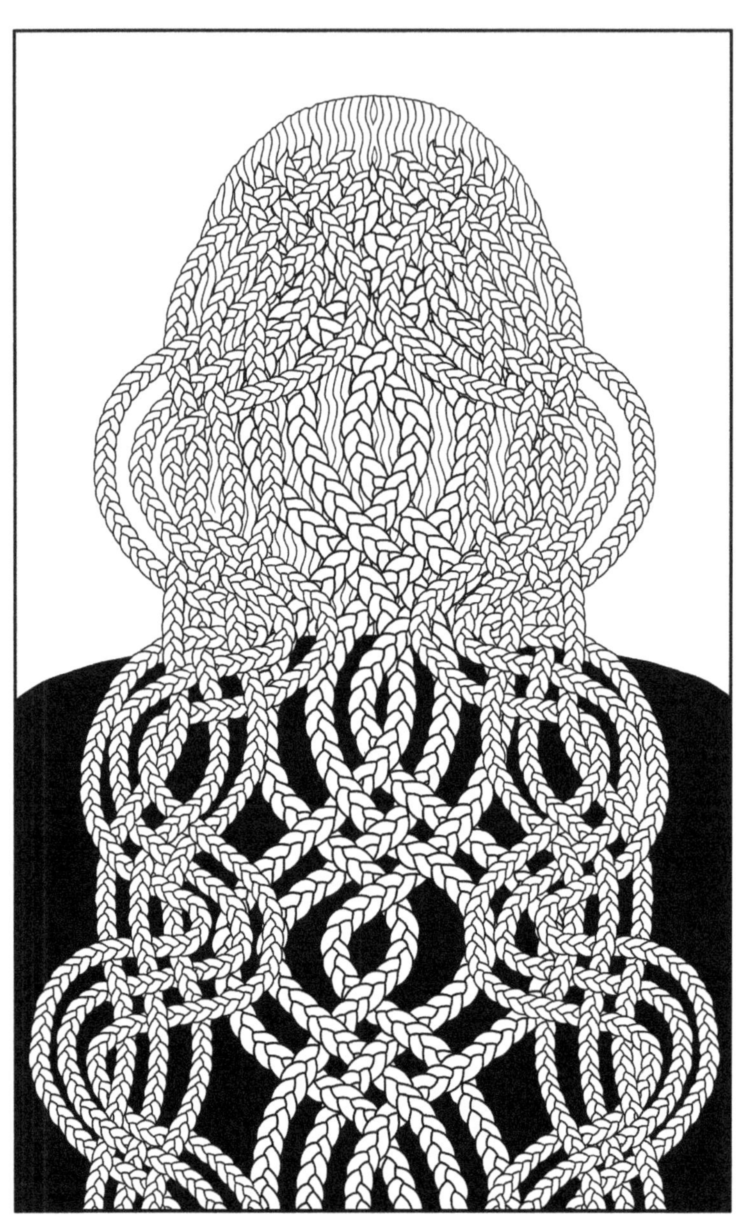

The Unforeseen Blessing

A thousand souls sit in darkness, each alone but unafraid. Time has no mean-ing, day and night the same. Voices call out to these souls, soft and insistent, but they do not answer. One by one, the hours pass within the quiet prison each has made of themselves, yet freedom is a handsbreadth away, if only they had the wisdom to reach across that mere illusion of distance.

—excerpt from The Chronicles of Disintegration

PAY NO ATTENTION TO my small jest. Such are the silly and frivolous thoughts that occur to one as buffeted by the disinterested tides of fortune as I.

Gathering myself, I began my tale. How my hand trembled as I recorded Mitra's death. How sweat broke upon my brow as I recalled the horrid worms and the even worse terror awaiting me on shore. With what gratitude did I write of the gilded child and Theda and the pair's timely and tender ministrations. With what awe did I attempt to describe those circles within circles, speaking them out in my mind, taking an inventory: the tower, the patio, the garden, the lawn. The wall, the marsh, the forest, the wheat. The cobblestone street and town beyond.

Then the cemetery and the high wall that prevented finding out if it was the outermost circumference or if other circles yet lay beyond. Was this place an island? Beyond the wall, I pictured a ring of tall cliffs which fell off to a circle of black sand that trickled into the sea, and once this image possessed me, it was hard to let it go.

I would ask my hosts the next time I saw them. One thing the recording of these events had shown me was that I'd been far too timid in asking questions. Whether I was afraid of the answers or not, it was past time I stopped being so passive as to my circumstances—which was all well and good, but what if my hosts never appeared to me again?

That was the question which burned at the forefront of my mind as I wrote through the long hours of the night, scarcely catching up to the current moment in my diary before the light of dawn arrived in the window. No one had come to me since I awoke in the tower, though obviously someone had brought me there, and my wounds had been tended.

But no meals had materialized, and regular feeding had been a hallmark of my visit here and my hosts' hospitality. Feeling bereft and even frightened, I set aside my pen and journal, only then realizing how cramped and painful my hand was from writing. Soot jumped down from where he had spent the night curled beside me in bed and trotted to the door, looking back at me confidently.

"You have the right of it, Soot," I said. "Today, we will be bold and brave. We'll take matters into our own hands (or paws, pardon) and stop relying upon the beneficence and indulgence of others."

It was awkward with only one hand, and I had to remove the sling to accomplish it, but I managed to wash myself and perform the other necessary morning rituals which must be gone through if one wished to keep oneself decent for viewing. I suppose others in my situation might have been less punctilious, but I have always prided myself on keeping up my personal standards regardless of circumstance.

I traded my soiled linen outfit for a clean one (of which there was always one, but only one, in the wardrobe). This ensemble was an even darker grey. It was much more complimentary to my pale skin than the lighter colors I had worn previously, so I didn't mind the change. The last step was to don the sling again, which I did most clumsily.

Leaving my chamber, I first stopped at the bookbindery, knocking before entering, but the room was empty and still. I thought about exploring the other floors but decided to check the places I was familiar with first. I was anxious to find one or the other of my hosts and seek some explanation of what had happened at the church, and how I had been returned to their care. The library was similarly bare of company, so I continued down to the parlor, which was just as quiet.

Stepping out onto the patio, I was relieved to find on the wrought-iron table a tray laden with dishes I assumed were meant for me and Soot. We ate gratefully while entertained by the various inhabitants of the garden: small songbirds which landed on flower heads, plucking seeds; bees and wasps, showy butterflies and drab moths flittering quickly from place to place; a variety of small lizards, green and brown and grey, skittering out onto the patio to drink up the warmth of the sun; and at the edge, where flower met stone, a small toad that blinked, singing a high trilling melody from time to time that was answered near and far by others of its kind.

Such a lovely and peaceful scene! I was sorry I'd neglected to bring my journal downstairs with me, for I would have liked to make sketches of some of these charming but transitory vignettes. I debated going back upstairs to fetch it but decided locating my hosts was of greater import.

On impulse, I decided to circumnavigate the base of the tower as I had not yet made a complete circuit of the exterior. I noticed that while the garden continued, the composition of flowers and plants changed subtly. The blooms grew both darker and richer in color and more exotic—plants with twisted stems and branches, oversized blooms which were somehow disturbing in their lushness and opulence. The air grew cooler too as the tower blocked the rays of the still rising sun.

I was so absorbed in examining the garden and the ever-changing interplay of light and shadow that I did not at first notice I was no longer alone. A soft sigh at my back startled me. It was Theda, seated with its hair pooled all around and mingling with a puddle at its feet. Sigh followed sigh, and I was taken aback to see water trickling down its body, giving the impression of weeping (though its face was as obscure as ever, so I could not be certain).

Unsure if I was welcome in such a private moment, I made a graceless, bobbing little bow and backed away in confusion. One gloved hand beckoned me forward, though Theda seemed too overcome to speak. When I drew near enough, it grasped my damaged arm, removing the sling over my head and unraveling the bandages. The revealed skin was pristine, and my arm and hand moved with as much vigor and mobility as they ever had.

What did it mean? Had I been unconscious longer than I thought? Such must be the case if I was so completely healed. Remembering my resolution to be more forthright, I almost asked, but something of the melancholy which lay about Theda, both visibly and in some intangible atmosphere that weighed heavily upon us, convinced me to postpone my curiosity once again.

Its heavy hair was soaked through and looked so uncomfortable that before I knew it, my hands reached out to it. My sister had taught me to braid and dress her hair for those occasions when her maid was indisposed, a task I had enjoyed and a skill which came back to me readily. Tentatively at first, not wanting to impose or offend, but then more confidently and quickly when no sign of protest was forthcoming, I divided the heavy locks into sections, twisting each into long braids which I then braided together again to form thicker plaits.

As I worked, the water slowly ceased, and Theda sat up straighter as though a burden was being lifted from its shoulders. More and more of the clothing beneath the hair became exposed. A shapeless black robe or gown brushed the floor and had a high-necked collar and long sleeves which tucked into the ends of the gloves. If I had hoped to understand better what form was beneath the cloak of hair, this clothing concealed just as much, yet it felt a very intimate gesture to touch and see even this which was usually hidden.

An emotion I couldn't identify welled up in me as I worked. Before long, I fell to weeping myself, great gusts of half-choked breath and wails expelled from the depths of my being. Blinded by tears, I worked by touch alone to finish my task. When the smaller sections were done, I gathered all together for one final braid, a pulsing, twisting, complicated animal of hair which slunk down Theda's back and curled around its ankles.

When I was done, gloved hands wiped my cheeks. That alien face, never still, never truly seen, leant toward mine and bestowed upon my forehead a kiss both hard and soft, tender and harsh, welcome and unwelcome, as cold as the first touch of snow and as warm as a bonfire whose flames have flown high to greet the midwinter moon.

"Thank you, Avery Mothmere."

THE FOREST REFUGE

I used to think it was inevitable and quite commonplace. Two hearts meeting, souls delighting in discovery and wonder. But now I understand it is the merest, slightest chance. Some lovers collide, fate-touched, and sparks fly, but untold multitudes pass each other in a crowd and never know what they have so narrowly missed. What unbounded joy they might have possessed.

—excerpt from Memoirs of a Disgraced Magician

CONFUSED AND UNEXPECTEDLY OPPRESSED by both gesture and words, I did something I'm not pleased nor proud to report: I turned and walked briskly away (though some ungenerous observer might describe it as more of a trot or canter). No voice called me back but my own conscience, for I knew at once I was being unforgivably rude. But I could not remain there one minute more, or I might explode or transform—into what, I couldn't say, but every part of my body tingled and complained. Whether with pain or pleasure, who could tell?

Before I knew it, I'd completed a half-circuit of the tower and was back again at my starting point. Panicked and disordered, too embarrassed to risk meeting Anchor or, even worse, Theda again while I was in such a state, I strode quickly past garden, lawn, wall and marshlands, losing myself in the shady forest where the air was cool and refreshing against my flushed and burning cheeks.

Feeling like a callow fool, unsophisticated, and much younger than my actual years, I suffered again and again as I replayed the scene in my imagination. I'd known many boon companions in my time, Mitra being only the latest. Jin and Roshan, Hart and Tahral—the names flitted through my mind with images of places and times closely entwined with the conjuration of these ghosts from the past. Was what I shared with any of these what romantics like to refer to as love? I'd thought so with every new relationship and regretted their endings, but now I wasn't so certain.

None of them had moved me, even over long acquaintance, as much as that solitary moment just passed. Was I in love with Theda? Was it even possible to be in love with such a being? It was at best presumptuous and at worst, absurd. And as for any notion such an emotion would be reciprocated, it was unthinkable. I did not understand what Theda was, but that it was in every way superior to my humble self was indisputable.

"Alien" I had termed its face, but this was a word I intended in its most complimentary form. Alien, exquisite, otherworldly. Existing on some plane I could never aspire to. Rather than love, it was more likely awe. A kind of adoration, as a believer might worship at the feet of their god. And Theda, no doubt, felt nothing but a kind indulgence towards me, as though I was an injured bird discovered in the garden and nursed back to health. An interesting novelty (which I knew to be much valued here), but there is no pride to be taken in simply existing as a new thing, an unexpected guest where such are few and far between.

As these thoughts raced through my mind, I stood still but for my panting breath, balanced on my feet like a startled deer, ready to run at the first sign of danger. For once, Soot was not anywhere I could see, and I spared a moment's concern before deciding he was well able to look after himself. My heart raced on. I lifted a hand to my forehead, all too aware of the exact spot where Theda's blessing had landed. I chided myself for reading so much into what was undoubtedly meant as a simple acknowledgement of a service rendered, as you or I might shake a proffered hand in thanks.

I had no wish to proceed to town and endure the necessity of engaging in mundane conversation with anyone I met there, yet I was still too mortified to return to the tower. I decided (or rather, my feet did—I cannot recall having any say in the matter) to wander the forest for a time. It had the advantage of being cooler there and full of distractions in the form of wildlife and plants which were not completely unfamiliar. Of all the places I'd been since washing ashore, this was the one most like the country where I had grown up.

I made mental notes on the many pleasant encounters I had with forest inhabitants both big (a red fox that watched me warily a moment before continuing on their way) and small (a shiny green beetle that flew past my face before landing on a tree branch). I regretted again leaving my journal behind. I would have to get back into the habit of carrying it with me, the easier to make accurate sketches of all I saw.

The shadow I'd sensed so often in this land stalked me here as well, but I had given up the game of looking behind me, trying to glimpse its form or ask what it wanted. It was far too cagey and wise to be caught out by such simple maneuvers. I wondered idly if I would ever meet it face to face, and whether that encounter would be to my advantage or my peril, but such was my general agitation that this was only of minor concern. It must wait its turn behind more pressing anxieties.

I'd been walking for some time when I came upon a figure seated cross-legged with eyes closed. It was Zaza. The giant looked content and relaxed, and I will admit I envied her serenity, possessing but little at that moment myself. She opened one eye at my approach, though I had tried to be quiet. I suppose when one has lived in the forest as long as she claimed, its sounds must be so familiar to you that any anomaly is conspicuous.

"It be the moth, don't it?" she asked with so humorous an air and friendly a grin that I assumed this was her version of a light joke, rather than forgetfulness as to my real name. "Come along and sit aside me. Trouble weighs upon you."

Unable to deny the truth of this assessment, I sat across from the giant, attempting as best I could to mirror their own posture though it did not come naturally to me.

"Close your eyes, breathe deep. Clear your mind and hark to the song of the forest. Let the trees speak to you. They've many and many a tale of ancient wonder that must delight us what take the time to truly hear."

I felt foolish, but since I had an audience of one, and she also had her eyes closed, I followed these instructions. I anticipated I would be unable to calm my thoughts, and was correct, at least at first. But the longer we sat, the more the hum and bustle of the forest invaded my mind, crowding out the worst of my internal clamor. My heart slowed, and I became aware of the pulsing of blood through my veins. The beauty of breathing, and the miracle of my body, for all its faults and injury, and how it had served me faithfully through the many years of my life.

After a long time, the giant spoke again. "There, ain't that better? Now, tell me your tale. A worry shared is a worry cut in half."

It was a poor recompense for the peace she had given me to lay my troubles upon her, but she seemed so in earnest that I found myself blurting out a litany of my unease, my questions, and my fears in a jumbled and confused barrage which could only have been half-comprehensible to anyone but myself.

When I had wound down like a dying clock, I expected... I don't know what. Answers to my questions, or at least some indication of whether I was mad or not. Though if I was and the giant was part of my delusions, I'm not sure any reassurance from her would have counted or comforted.

Instead, the only part of my convoluted tale which interested her was my attentions to Theda with the braiding of its hair.

"Now that be a great kindness! A great kindness—and Theda has known little enough of that," was all she said.

And though I repeated my questions and even asked what she meant by this, no other reassurance was forthcoming.

THE SACRED INTERLUDE

Spirits are tethered to this world by ghostly bonds as thin as a gossamer thread and as flimsy as a plucked feather. Yet pound for pound, silk is stronger than steel and feathers enable the miracle of flight. Who is to say these bonds that tie the departed to this plane are not just as wondrous and worthy of our admiration and study?

    –excerpt from A Grimoire Malign

DETERMINED TO AT LEAST get some idea of whether whatever emotion I held for Theda might be reciprocated, I asked whether Theda had ever loved.

Zaza laughed, long and low. "Theda loves everybody Theda visits, and Theda visits everybody, soon or late."

With this extraordinary and extraordinarily unhelpful observation, the giant lumbered to her feet, pulling herself up with the assistance of the tree trunks and branches surrounding us. "You think too much and too often and of too many things, little moth. Devote as much time to feeling as you do to thinking and you may have a chance."

A chance at what, I was not to discover, for she strode away then with nary a glance back at me.

She was not the first to give me such advice. I was over-analytical in my approach to life. Spontaneity, impulse, emotion were all foreign to my nature. This often put me at odds with the rest of humanity, or at least, so it felt. I did not show affection easily or openly. Perhaps neither did Theda, for if it did love everyone it met, I had not sensed more than mild interest and kindly consideration during our interactions. At least until that chilly kiss.

I had to catch myself there, for what were these musings but overthinking again as the giant had accused? Curling up between the roots of one of the trees, I tried to calm my mind again and simply exist and relax. I succeeded well enough to fall asleep—not surprising given I'd stayed up all night writing. When I awoke, I judged it to be late afternoon by the quality of the light, and my stomach was complaining of having missed a noon repast.

I thought briefly of continuing on to town and exchanging another story for one of Jack Scrabbin's pies but knew this was simple cowardice. Best to return to the tower and face Theda and get any awkwardness over with as quickly as possible. Looking about in dismay, I realized I had no idea which direction to go. A fluttering above my head betrayed the presence of the grey raven sitting on a branch and examining me.

"Hello, friend. Are you here to show me the way home?" I asked, realizing only as the words left my lips that this was a curious way to refer to the tower.

The raven hopped about a bit, then took wing, flying from branch to branch while always looking back to see if I was following. In this way, we made slow but steady progress until we were at the marshlands again. Wishing to thank it for its repeated services as guide but having no food or shiny objects which might interest such a bird, I settled on a low bow instead which it solemnly returned.

I followed the boardwalk back to the wall where I found Soot waiting for me.

"You abandoned me, you faithless creature," I teased.

Soot simply yawned and jumped down upon the lawn, leading the way back to the tower with his tail held high like a standard at the front of a military parade.

On impulse, when we reached the garden, I plucked some of the choicest blooms here and there, creating an impromptu bouquet which I tied with the tough vine of a twisting plant. A poor gift to give one's host—flowers from their own garden—but since I was bereft of any possessions but the journal, pen, and ink, I hoped it would be seen as a gesture of goodwill and not as insult.

I found Theda upon the patio, seated at the wrought-iron table with a large bundle before it. Its hair was now dry and had been released from the braids, but their mark was still upon the locks, giving them a wavy pattern like ripples on the surface of a calm lake when some unseen creature is passing below.

"This is your shroud," Theda said, stroking the soft cloth. "Anchor fetched it from town. It is custom for a friend or family member to embroider your name upon it. I would be honored to do this service if you consider me a friend."

"I do, of course," I replied, placing my poor offering upon the table as I took a seat opposite. "I wish to apologize for my abrupt departure earlier. I—"

I paused, not sure how best to explain my unforgiveable behavior.

Theda spoke again. "I have known far worse in my time. One such as I expects nothing."

"But that isn't right!" I protested. "You deserve as much courtesy as any other."

"It is generous to say so," it said, picking up the bouquet and bringing the flowers close to its ever-flickering face, "but you do not yet comprehend the entire truth of me. When you discover it, you will understand."

Setting aside an almost paralyzing feeling of shyness, I bravely asserted, "I look forward to gaining such an understanding. In fact, I think I desire it more than anything else I have ever wished for in life."

A gloved hand reached out and covered one of my own. "It is better you do not understand. Not yet. Let us have this interlude where you imagine you could love me, and I imagine I could be loved. A precious pretense. The most exquisite conceit which has happened to me at any time within memory. I will cling to it a little longer if you allow."

Moved beyond measure yet unsure how to answer this touching but puzzling plea, I simply nodded. I didn't wish to risk upsetting Theda any further after my earlier rudeness, so I also let die unasked the dozen or more questions I'd been determined to have answered before this day was over.

We dwelled instead in companionable quiet, hand in hand, as the sun set and the sky took on the unique shade of blue-purple-black seen at no other time than twilight. Stars twinkled to life. I watched them idly, looking for familiar constellations but finding none. Anchor joined us, dancing under the night sky. Sparks flew off from their golden, papery skin and wafted ever upward until they disappeared, quenched by time or distance.

I felt that this otherworld I had entered through shipwreck and misfortune was holding its breath. An interlude, as Theda had said, that would not last long nor ever come again. And for once, I did not anticipate or plan or worry or question. I simply was.

The Headlong Flight

Some days are demonstrably longer than others. The hours pass more slowly, minutes crawl and seconds saunter. Why does time slow for hard things? And speed by the moments you want to hold and savor? Time can be a cruel and arbitrary god—I wish I knew what offering to give to make it behave.
—excerpt from Memoirs of a Disgraced Magician

I WAS HARD-PRESSED TO write sensibly of the day's events in my journal during the wee hours of the night when we three finally parted. I settled for sketching out Theda as best I could, with its hair braided, the shapeless form, the indecipherable face. Was it possible to love what could not be seen?

Glad I was to drift off to sleep and rest again from ceaseless pondering upon obscure mysteries. I was wrenched awake by a sharp knock upon the door which seemed to require an answer. No such formalities had been in evidence in the past, so it was with some trepidation that I arose and responded to the summons by opening the door.

There stood the gilded child. They thrust a change of outfit in my face with the words, "We must hurry!"

Showing no signs of departing, they stood watching me, shifting from one foot to another with every symptom of distress and impatience.

Alarmed and concerned by this unprecedented behavior, I rushed through my morning routine and changed (not without some acute self-consciousness before an audience) into my day's clothing. These were the darkest-hued I had been given yet—a blue-grey so deep as to appear nearly black, yet the shape was much the same: loose-fitting trousers and a sleeveless top.

As soon as I was dressed, the child clasped my hand and pulled me down the stairs. Soot bounded after us at some pains to keep up, such was our heedless haste. Given my tendency to clumsiness, I was relieved to make it to the bottom of the steps without incident. Theda was nowhere in sight, and neither was breakfast on the patio.

Goaded on by Anchor and too out of breath from our precipitous descent to shout a question, I simply followed, stumbling and struggling to maintain the punishing pace being set by the child. They were so unlike their usual tranquil self. Even their shine was dulled, like some internal fire was in the process of being quenched.

Through the garden we ran and across the lawn. A vault over the wall and sprint along the boardwalk over the marsh followed. When we reached the edge of the forest, a most extraordinary thing! The child transformed before my eyes into the golden stag and knelt before me, prodding me painfully with the tip of a black antler until I mounted its back. Soot leapt upon my lap, and we were off on a terrifying gallop through the thick trees, with me sure of disaster at any moment.

It was then that I thought I must be dreaming, for how could the child and the stag be one and the same? Absurd! *But—was it?* my traitor brain asked. Was it any more absurd or unlikely than any other of my experiences? I hardly had time to ponder this conundrum before I was flung off onto the ground at the edge of the forest.

The child reappeared and grabbed my hand, attempting to pull me to my feet and make off with me again. Tired and sore and bewildered at the urgency of their actions, I stubbornly held my ground until they began to drag me, which was both painful and undignified and reminded me disturbingly of my ordeal in the church. I pulled my hand free long enough to get to my feet, puffing out, "Go! Go if you must! I swear I will follow as quickly as I'm able."

Anchor gave me what I would term a hard look, then nodded once, twice and was off. I did my best to keep my word though my ribs ached from trying to catch my breath.

The wheat field seemed to stretch forever, but we did finally gain the cobblestone street. The child kept up the pace, careening down the sidewalk, counter-clockwise, with impetuous speed. It must have still been early in the day, for there were signs the town was only now coming to life. There were enough citizens out and about, however, that I thought surely our strange flight must attract attention and speculation.

I scarcely had the time or wits to gaze around me, but I did send beseeching looks here and there to see if someone might offer some explanation or assistance for my plight. However, everywhere I looked, people avoided my eyes—even Jack Scrabbin, who was already up and offering his wares. I must have been well-addled because I could have sworn I saw the Captain striding through the crowd at distance, or if not, his twin. What a miracle if more than I had survived the wreck! I was frustrated beyond measure that I was not currently at liberty to investigate further.

The child finally found the alleyway they had been looking for, impatiently beckoning to me and Soot, who had gamely kept up with the race, though his poor sides were heaving as heavily as my own. We followed Anchor and found ourselves again at the cemetery, though today it was empty of mourners. I could not help, even in my distressed state, admiring again the perfect symmetry and order with which the gravestones were laid out. It was most pleasing to the eye—quite a work of art and planning.

And then we were there, at the impenetrable wall—yet not so today. Today a passageway stood, a set of wooden doors, carved deeply with a similar geometric design as the door to my bedchamber, though larger and more elaborately detailed. The doorknobs were hand-shaped, reaching out as though to snatch at us. The child grasped one and pulled my hand forward until I was forced to do the same with the other.

With what disgust did I feel that hand clasp mine. It was unpleasantly oily, leathery-sharp, and toothy. It gripped me so painfully that I cried out as the doors flung wide and we were pulled violently through them. Soot was either not fast enough or not welcome, for he was shut upon the other side of the wall. His howls and cries in protest of our separation were pitiful to hear.

Our hectic race apparently at its finish line, Anchor came to a halt, standing so still that for a moment they looked like a golden statue. I glanced around, curious despite my fright to finally glimpse what was beyond the outer wall but was disappointed to find that a heavy fog lay all around us, making it impossible to see more than a few feet in any direction.

"Now what?" I asked when I had regained enough breath to speak. "What is going on? Where is Theda?"

"Forget Theda," the child said, pulling two things from—I would say pockets if it were clad in any normal raiment, but instead, it produced these objects from cracks in its skin, in between the fiery, papery layers of it.

The first item was my journal, which they thrust into my hands. The front cover opened and the pages within turned of their own accord, beginning with my own familiar handwriting. But then page after blank page appeared and was instantly filled with writing and drawings that I caught but a glimpse of before the page was turned again. It was as if my future history and experiences were being written all in a moment and would soon fill the book completely, leaving no room for any other.

The second item the child produced was even more sinister than the first. Pulling it out of their skin, bit by bit in endless measure, much as I had once in my childhood seen a cheap conjurer produce an endless silk scarf from their sleeve, the dark cloth pooled around my feet and my name appeared, picked out elegantly in silver thread. It was my shroud.

THE FINAL VOYAGE

And then the passenger spoke again: "Sometimes, death comes not as a curse but a blessed relief. Give over those oars to me, Ferryman, and I will gladly row this final journey." And this was the reply: "A generous offer that I will accept. It is a rare pleasure to sit back and enjoy the scenery. I never noticed before how beautiful the flames are upon the water."

 –excerpt from A Grimoire Malign

A CHILL RAN THROUGH my marrow at the sight, for what use is a shroud to any but the dead? Did the child mean to kill me? Had I offended them or made them jealous of my connection with their housemate? After all, they had known Theda far longer than I. It was presumptuous of me to force myself into their contented companionship, a disruptive force however much I might wish not to be.

 "What is this?" I asked, poking gingerly at the cloth with my foot.

 "You will have need of it. It is cold crossing the waters. This idyll is ended."

 "By whose decision?"

 "By necessity. There is no future, here or elsewhere."

I would have protested, but the pages of my journal began to flutter and tremble, ripping themselves from the beautiful binding and wrapping themselves around me. I tried to strip them away, but they clung too tightly, sticky as flypaper—only I was the fly trapped within. The paper slowly dissolved and somehow took my clothing with it, for when all was done, I was naked except for the words and drawings of the book, etched upon every surface of me like a sailor's tattoos.

And yet this was not the end of my transformation, for when the paper had vanished, the shroud cloth rose to take its place, snaking round me and pouring itself over my body like paint. Before I could fully comprehend what was happening or attempt to resist, every inch of my skin was transmogrified into the deep purple-black shroud, and the words *Avery Mothmere* shone out for all to read in silver thread across my chest.

I cannot describe the suffocating feeling of being so embraced by the awful shroud—I could only imagine it was something like awakening in a coffin, six feet deep, after a premature burial. The claustrophobic terror, the futile but desperate attempts at escape, the panic which would tip any but the strongest minds over into madness.

Anchor gave me a look that was not, I would say, unsympathetic to my distress, but they were committed to some path and were not to be turned aside or appealed to. They waved one arm and the fog parted, revealing a dark sandy soil, bare of any vegetation. Taking me by one hand, they led me again, but more gently and slowly this time as though the need for haste was past. I could not move or walk within the shroud but simply floated and bobbed like a child's balloon beside my guide.

I could see we were approaching what looked to be a lake or river, for I could make out some kind of land on the far shore. The water was murky and impenetrable to sight, though shivers along the surface hinted there might be creatures hidden below. A simple wooden rowboat was beached upon the near shore, and I knew at once that Anchor meant to place me in it, for it was the exact image of the boat from the journal's gilded decoration—a prediction of the future rather than a memory of the past.

The fathomless horror which filled me at the idea was out of proportion to the mundanity of the vessel. It looked much worn—antique even—with two plank benches, one meant for the oarsman, I presumed, and one for their passenger. The oars must be for Anchor to wield, unless another appeared, or they somehow expected me to row in my constricted condition.

Nearly-forgotten lessons sprang to mind. Old myths translated from an ancient tongue by our tutor, as my sister drummed her heels against her chair (always so easily bored and impatient with our school hours in a way that I—the scholar, the scientist—was not).

These memories flowed back to me now. Tales of a ferryman and coins exchanged for a final voyage. The name Theda had bestowed upon the gilded child no longer seemed arbitrary or odd, though I cursed myself that I'd failed to understand the significance of this clue when it might have done me some good.

"I'm afraid we cannot embark, for I have no money to pay the fare," I murmured, half in jest, still resisting the idea that any of this was more than a dream.

Anchor said nothing but ripped two patches of golden skin from their forearm and placed them upon my eyes, blinding me. I felt the warmth and lightness of the paper solidify into the cold, heavy metal of coin as my body was placed upon a bench in the boat. When the weight was lifted from my eyes, I saw the child, seated opposite me with hand outstretched, two golden coins—my fare—upon their palm. As I watched, the coins were transmuted and absorbed back into the child's skin like they had never been.

They placed their hands upon the oars, and though they made no other movement or effort, the boat began to glide straight across the water to whatever lay on the other side. I'd no wish to discover what awaited us there but had no choice. Even if I found a way to free myself from the shroud, the doors through the wall had closed and sealed behind us. The way back to the tower was lost to me, and I sensed there was nothing on the barren, foggy shore we had just left to sustain me if I was trapped there.

A sense of ennui overcame me as I considered the possibilities. This was a dream... or I was mad... or sick with fever and hallucinating... or...

My mind shied away from articulating the last option, but it came unbidden just the same: I was dead already, or at the very least, on the verge of crossing that narrow threshold which separates one state of being from the next. This was to be my final voyage.

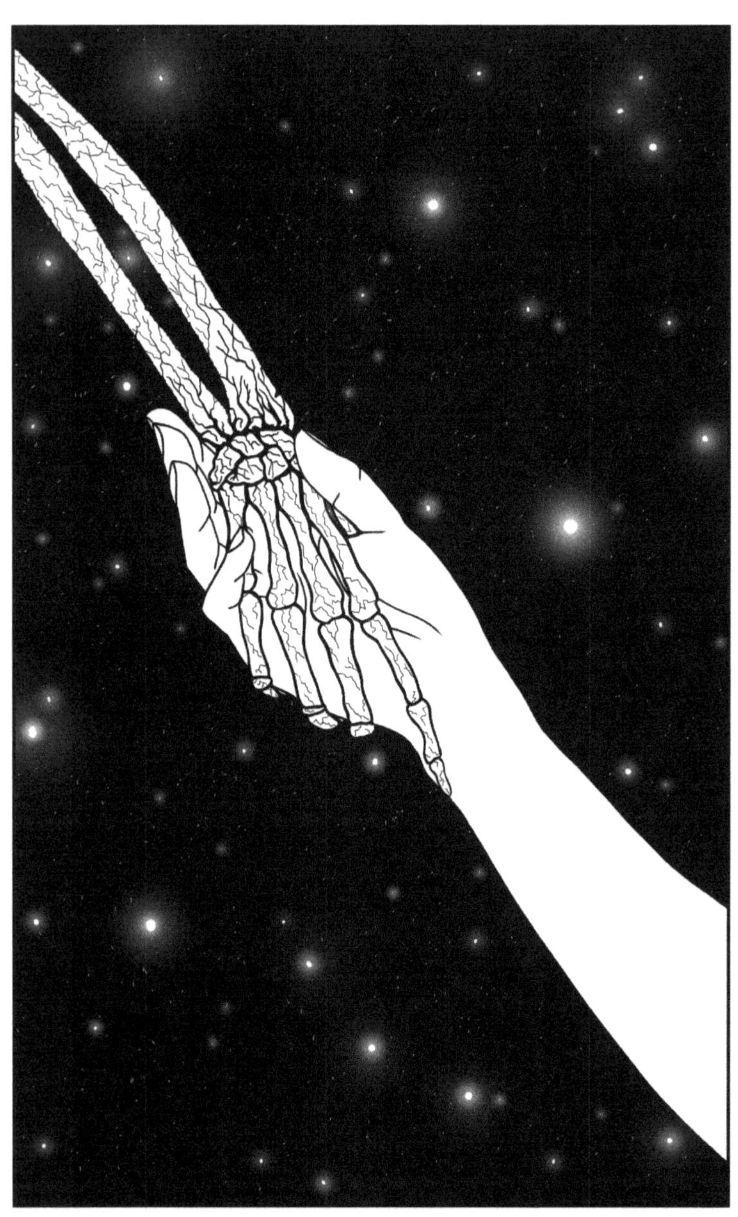

The True End

Lay our weary bones upon a lonely shore so that we may see the sky, hand in hand. We will count the ancient stars as they smile down upon us and bathe us in their kindly light. Let the shifting sands beneath our backs burnish us up until not one bit is left of what we were but our immortal souls. Then watch them soar and flutter and swirl in an endless murmuration of exultation.

—excerpt from page torn from Avery Mothmere's diary

I WAS NOT A religious person and had ruminated only idly and rarely upon speculations of the afterlife. To my scientific mind, when the mechanical processes which sustain life came to a stop, through whatever cause, a body becomes a thing, an organism to be returned to the earth and so continue to nurture the cycle of life and death that sustains our world.

Did I believe in the soul? I thought what some would term that could be more accurately described as personality—the sum of education, experience, emotions, and intellect which made up what we would call "ourself" and set us apart from our fellows. These were my logical, rational, and level-headed beliefs, and though I might enjoy a well-written tale of a haunting or entertain pleasantly morbid imaginings from time to time, such was the totality of my thoughts upon the subject.

But now, what was I to believe? It was hubris to think I could know anything about a topic which could not be fully investigated—for the few test subjects who had been resuscitated, returned with only confused impressions and contradictory information. What a pity I could not record this journey in my destroyed journal. What a prize it would have been for scientists, philosophers, and religious scholars to pore over and argue and hypothesize.

Such were the reflections which occupied me as we sailed toward the distant shore. I strove to remain calm and maintain as much of a semblance of composure and dignity as was possible under such unfavorable conditions. I remember being impressed with how silent it was. Neither the boat nor the water made any sound as we traveled, which made it only the more disquieting to suddenly hear the agitated flapping of wings overhead.

I looked up and spied the grey raven from the forest keeping pace with the boat. Anchor followed my gaze, making a *tch-tch* sound which I interpreted as annoyance. Perhaps the bird did not belong here and was trespassing, but I, for one, was grateful to see it. My heart leapt at this reminder of life and nature and—a friend? (For I recalled how kind and helpful the raven had ever been to me.)

It passed us by, alighting in the distance on the fast-approaching shore. Far quicker than I would have liked, we joined it there, the boat gliding smoothly up upon the sands of yet another beach. Brilliant fires, many times taller than even the giant, Zaza, blazed here—though no smoke or ash could be seen. I was strangely chilled, grateful for the first time for the warmth of my shroud.

We disembarked, Anchor guiding me, still floating, from the boat. Of the raven, there was no sign, but a figure cloaked and hooded all in black was there to greet us. One boney hand grasped a long-handled scythe made of the same mahogany wood that had become so familiar in this place. The other boney hand pushed back the hood to reveal a skull with empty hollows where the eyes should be.

And then the cloak was shrugged aside entirely to reveal an elegant skeleton, white bones shining and flickering in the light from the fires with an incandescent beauty.

"Be not afraid, Avery Mothmere," it said.

It swung its dreaded blade at me, cutting my shroud in twain with a single, delicate stroke. The suffocating cloth released its hold upon me and fell at my feet, while the black ink faded from my skin, leaving us two to face each other unadorned with any raiment or disguise but our own true selves.

"I am not afraid, Theda. Host. Healer. The shadow that watches over me. Grey raven guide and keeper of my heart. I see you, my own, my beloved."

AND SO WE REACH the end of my tale.

But what happened next, you ask? An understandable curiosity—for there are not many love stories such as ours—but there really is not much more to say. I saw my dearest one revealed and did not turn away, but instead delighted in its rightful form and the trust it showed in showing me.

The gilded child apologized for their attempt to hurry me along my journey and save their associate and friend from possible rejection and hurt. They re-constituted the pages of my journal and mended it so skillfully that you would never guess it had once been utterly destroyed (as whoever has taken the trouble to decipher and transcribe my scrawls herein can attest).

We returned that fateful day to the tower, picking up a much-ruffled black cat along the way, and there we existed in peace and with a deep contentment such as I'd never known or thought possible. I was not of much practical help for Theda's eternal responsibilities and the grief they caused that sensitive soul, but I liked to think—no, I was sure that my own unselfish dedication was as a healing balm upon the wound and kept utter despair at bay.

You may imagine us seated on the patio as a purple-hued twilight falls. I have a stack of books on the table in front of me (for I have ambitions of studying every volume in our vast library now that I have time and leisure to do so). Soot lies curled upon my lap, asleep. The insects are buzzing their goodnights and tucking themselves into petaled beds. An owl serenades us with a hooting rhythm while the child waltzes among the flowers, golden sparks twirling off into the growing dark. We sit in perfect harmony, drinking in the scene.

I clasp a hand of sinew and bone—I know each crater and plane of it by heart—and we make a game of naming every star that appears above. And when we two are done at last, we begin the game again.

About the Author

Helen Whistberry (she/they) is the pen name for an indie author and artist who began writing after retiring from a long career working in libraries. They have published numerous books as well as contributing horror and fantasy stories to anthologies. Helen's writing often explores their own experiences with gender, asexuality, alienation, and autism. Their whimsical digital artwork focuses on the natural world. Helen also loves to read and review books by fellow indie and small press authors. You can find out more by visiting their website for a complete list of publications and links: https://www.helenwhistberry.com/

I hope you enjoyed this tale. If you have the time and inclination, reviews left on any of the major review sites are always greatly appreciated. Thank you so much for your support and for accompanying me on this writing and art journey.

Sign up for my newsletter to keep up to date with all my doings and receive a free ebook of my forest stories, The Melody of Trees! Link: https://BookHip.com/QVZXZGM

CHECK OUT MY OTHER BOOKS!

WHEN YOUR HEART IS A BROKEN THING

A lonely man shunned by society and haunted by a beautiful corpse. Sentient toys in a life and death struggle with unspeakable evil. Spectral visitations at midnight and in broad daylight. Fairy and folk tale re-imaginings full of eldritch places and events. Glimpses of the future and reminiscences of times past and times that never were and never will be. This generous selection of short stories encompasses genres from folk horror to dystopian sci fi, animal fantasy to ghost tales. Enter the imagination of Helen Whistberry and enjoy 19 unforgettable stories with the author's signature mix of horror and hope. Includes 20 original illustrations by the author. Link: https://books2read.com/ABrokenThing

ONCE UPON A WAVE OF WITCHES

(with co-author Eli Belt)

Amelia Arrowheart is a homebody. Beatrice Buttons most decidedly is not. When these two ladies of a certain age meet and become fast friends, neither expects the extraordinary challenges they will face together and apart. Welcome to Lichen, a place like no other, where fungi are revered, cloud creatures crowd the skies, and sea witches wield their power for the good of all. Two mischievous little boys, a space pirate, and a monster that reaches out from the depths of the ocean will change their lives forever. Join Beatrice and Amelia on the adventure of a lifetime as they take to the skies and plunge into the depths of the sea to save a friend and break a curse! A unique and uplifting fantasy tale celebrating friendship, loyalty, and love. Includes 33 original illustrations! Link: https://bo oks2read.com/WaveOfWitches

THE TAIL OF NIGHTSHADE

"A mouse scrabbled along under crisp, fallen leaves, whiskers twitching. Death, disguised as an owl, kept watch high above, unblinking eyes orbed bright in the moonlight…" Thus begins an adventure unlike any other for Nightshade, a young mouse who never expected to venture very far from their cozy burrow. Over the course of a few eventful days, they will meet strangers both weird and magnificent, including an impetuous bear and a lovely wyrm, a flitter-flutter and a whirligig, a wizard of modest talents and a legendarily monstrous cat, and a most wondrous being of light. Together they will navigate a noble quest, face unimaginable dangers, and experience astonishing events. Through it all, they will cling to the one thing they most believe: there is no obstacle that cannot be overcome if all remain true. Includes 31 original illustrations by the author. Link: https://books2read.com/TailOfNightshade

THE MELODY OF TREES

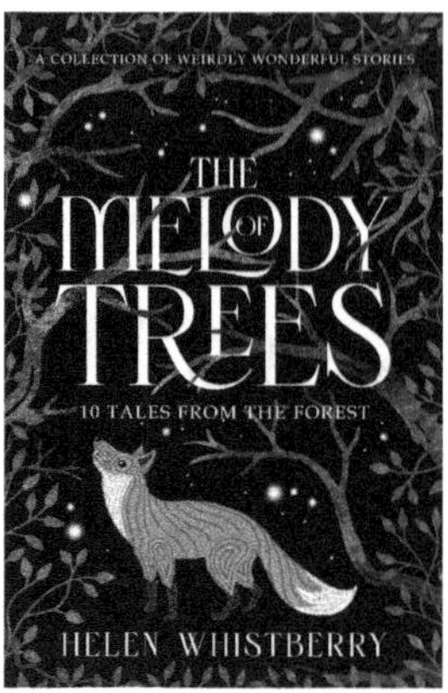

Experience the unforgettable magic of these original stories and illustrations. You'll discover an elder god keeping a loving eye on their forest, a girl made of glass and other characters fighting for their lives against both impossible odds and monsters (human and otherwise), some wise guys having a supernaturally bad day, and the exploits of a loner gun-for-hire and his loyal dragon. From fantasy and folklore to horror and sci-fi, these tales are tied together not only by their forest settings but by a sense of humanity (even in those characters who aren't quite human), empathy for all creatures, and the weird beauty to be found in moments both light and dark. Each story accompanied by an original illustration by the author. Link: https://books2read.com/MelodyOfTrees

THE JIM MALHAVEN MYSTERIES

Mystery series set in mid-America in the 1950s. Light noir with a cozy mystery feel and a touch of the paranormal that pays loving tribute to the wise guy detectives of the 40s and 50s. Jim Malhaven is a goodhearted but down on his luck reporter at a small-time newspaper. He often gets more than he bargains for when his editor shoots him some unusual assignments and as much as he tries to avoid the supernatural, it seems intent on tracking him down! The Malhaven Mysteries are meant to be lighthearted and humorous while still acknowledging the realities of the period and place it is set in. Some violence that is on the milder side compared to most modern day thrillers and no harsh language. Find the first in the series here: https://books2read.com/WeirdSisters

www.ingramcontent.com/pod-product-compliance
Lightning Source LLC
Chambersburg PA
CBHW070423310726

48977CB00003B/806